THE HARDY BOYS

Undercover Brothers®

PAPERCUTZ™

#1 "The Ocean of Osyria"

#2 "Identity Theft"

#3 "Mad House"

#4 "Malled"

#5 "Sea You, Sea Me!"

#6 "Hyde & Shriek"

#7 "The Opposite Numbers"

#8 "Board To Death"

#9 "To Die Or Not To Die?"

#10 "A Hardy Day's Night"

#11 "Abracadeath"

#12 "Dude Ranch O' Death!"

#13 "The Deadliest Stunt"

#14 "Haley Danelle's Top Eight!"

#15 "Live Free, Die Hardy!"

#16 "Shhhhhh!"

#17 "Word Up!"

#18 "D.A.N.G.E.R. Spells the Hangman"

Coming Soon! #19 "Chaos at 30,000 Feet!"

$7.95 each in paperback, $12.95 each in hardcover.

Please add $4.00 for postage and handling for the first book, add $1.00 for each additional book. Please make check payable to NBM Publishing. Send to: **Papercutz, 40 Exchange Place, Suite 1308, New York, NY 10005 • 1-800-886-1223 • www.papercutz.com**

THE HARDY BOYS

Undercover Brothers®

#18

D.A.N.G.E.R. Spells the Hangman

SCOTT LOBDELL • Writer

PAULO HENRIQUE MARCONDES • Artist

Based on the series by
FRANKLIN W. DIXON

PAPERCUTZ™

New York

D.A.N.G.E.R. Spells the Hangman
SCOTT LOBDELL — Writer
PAULO HENRIQUE MARCONDES — Artist
MARK LERER — Letterer
LAURIE E. SMITH — Colorist
CHRIS NELSON AND SHELLY DUTCHAK — Production
MICHAEL PETRANEK — Editorial Assistant
JIM SALICRUP
Editor-in-Chief

ISBN: 978-1-59707-160-4 paperback edition
ISBN: 978-1-59707-161-1 hardcover edition

Distributed by Macmillan

Printed in China June 2009
by New Era Printing Limited
Room 1101-1103, Trende Centre
29-31 Cheung Lee St
Chai Wan, Hong Kong

10 9 8 7 6 5 4 3 2 1

CHAPTER ONE: "PAINT THAT A SHAME!"

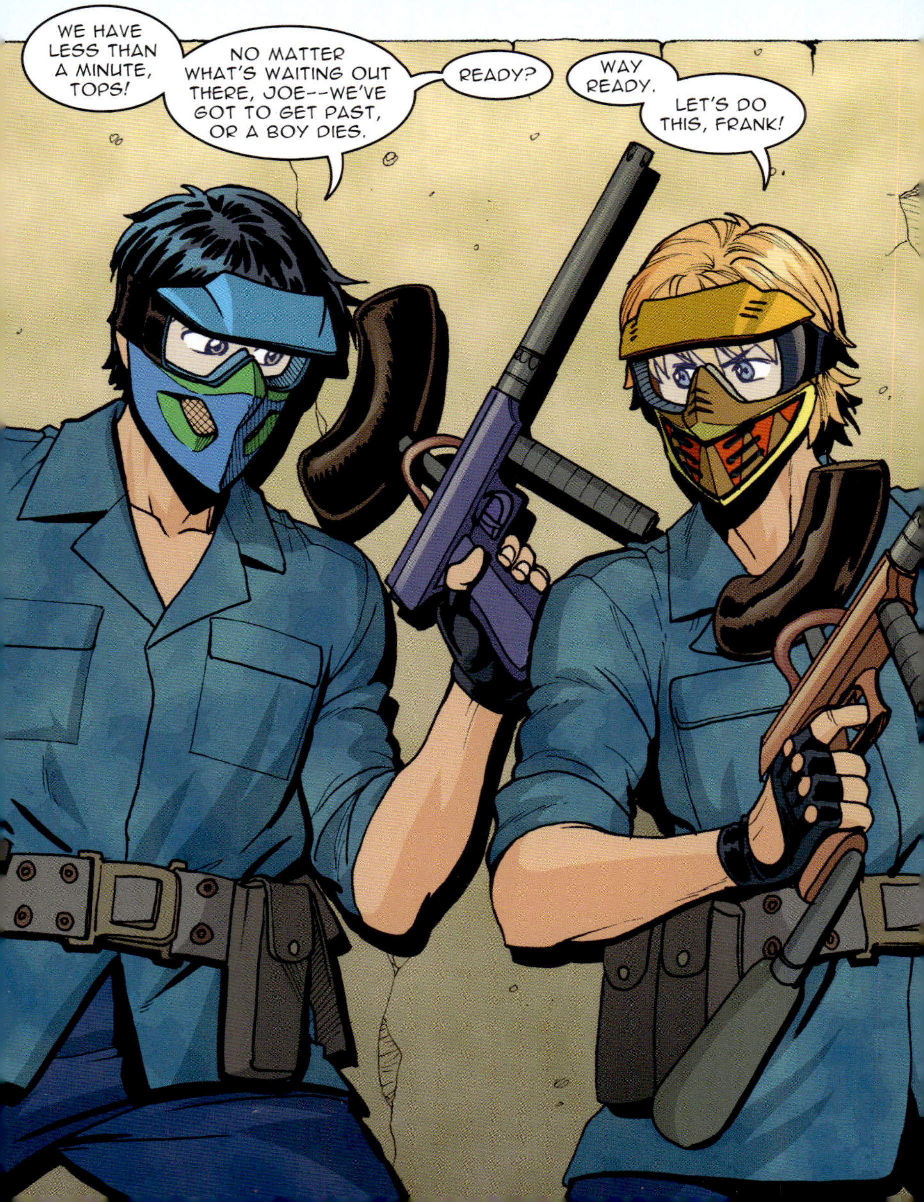
WE HAVE LESS THAN A MINUTE, TOPS!
NO MATTER WHAT'S WAITING OUT THERE, JOE--WE'VE GOT TO GET PAST, OR A BOY DIES.
READY?
WAY READY.
LET'S DO THIS, FRANK!

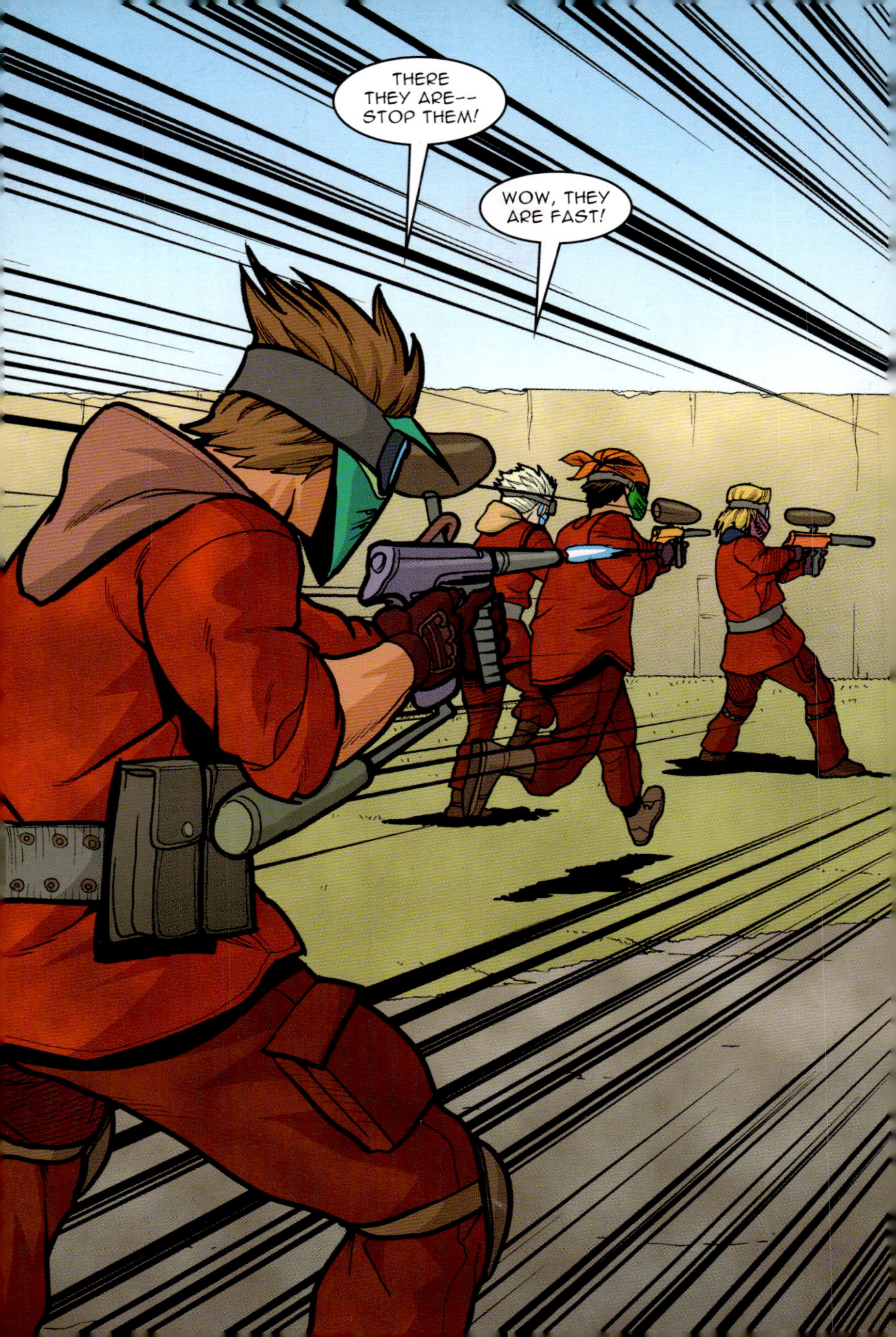
THERE THEY ARE-- STOP THEM!
WOW, THEY ARE FAST!

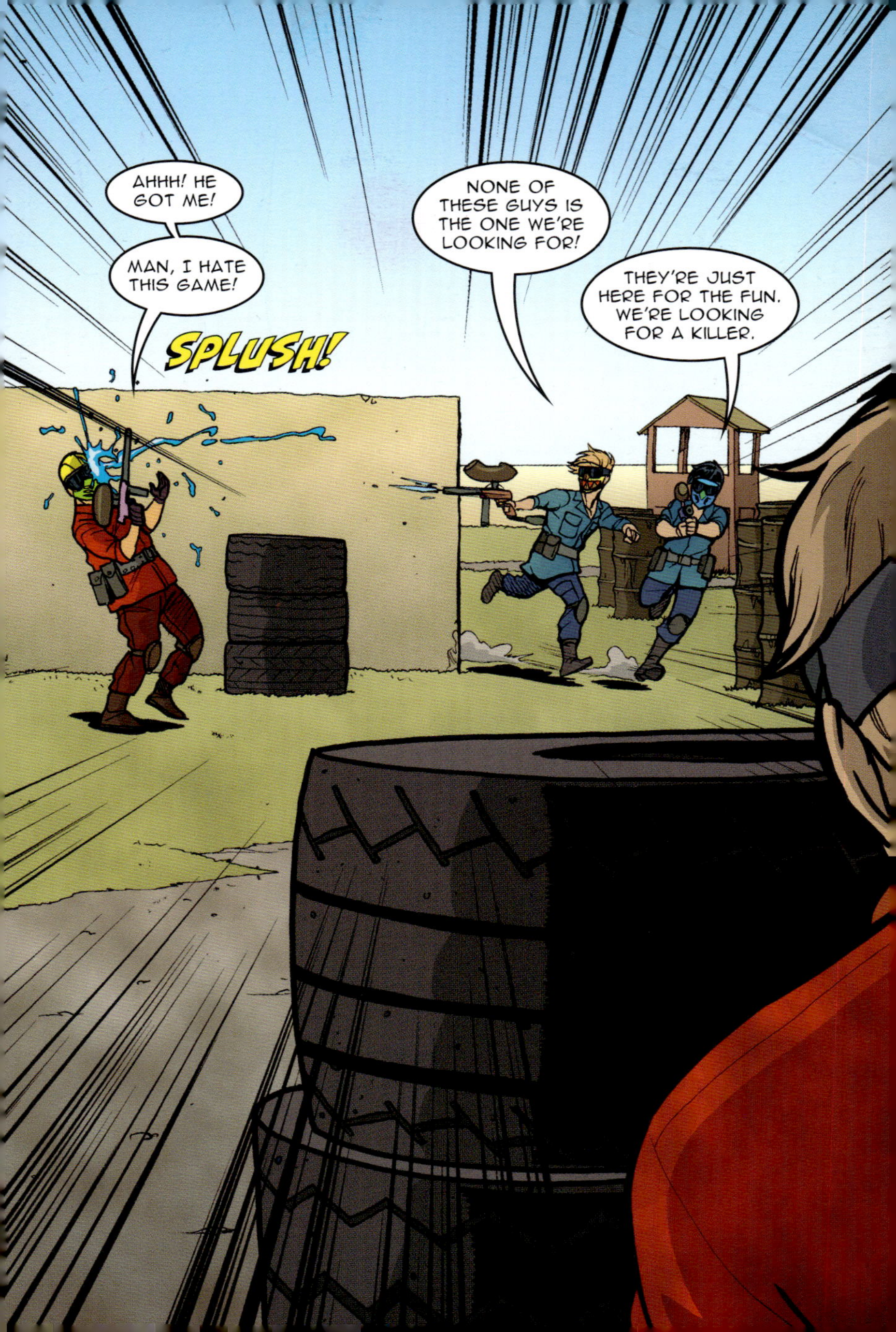
AHHH! HE GOT ME!
MAN, I HATE THIS GAME!
SPLUSH!
NONE OF THESE GUYS IS THE ONE WE'RE LOOKING FOR!
THEY'RE JUST HERE FOR THE FUN. WE'RE LOOKING FOR A KILLER.

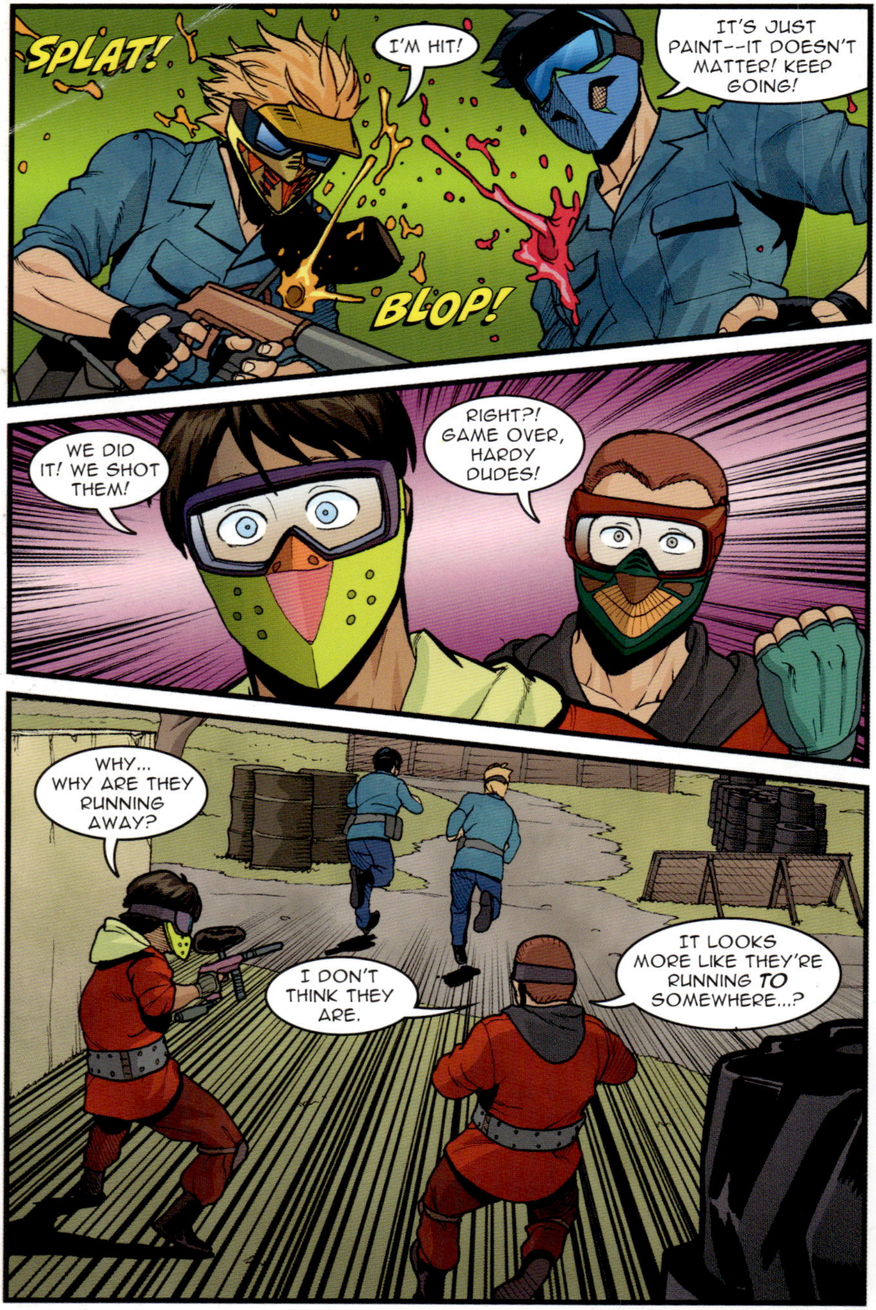
SPLAT!
I'M HIT!
IT'S JUST PAINT--IT DOESN'T MATTER! KEEP GOING!
BLOP!
WE DID IT! WE SHOT THEM!
RIGHT?! GAME OVER, HARDY DUDES!
WHY... WHY ARE THEY RUNNING AWAY?
I DON'T THINK THEY ARE.
IT LOOKS MORE LIKE THEY'RE RUNNING TO SOMEWHERE...?

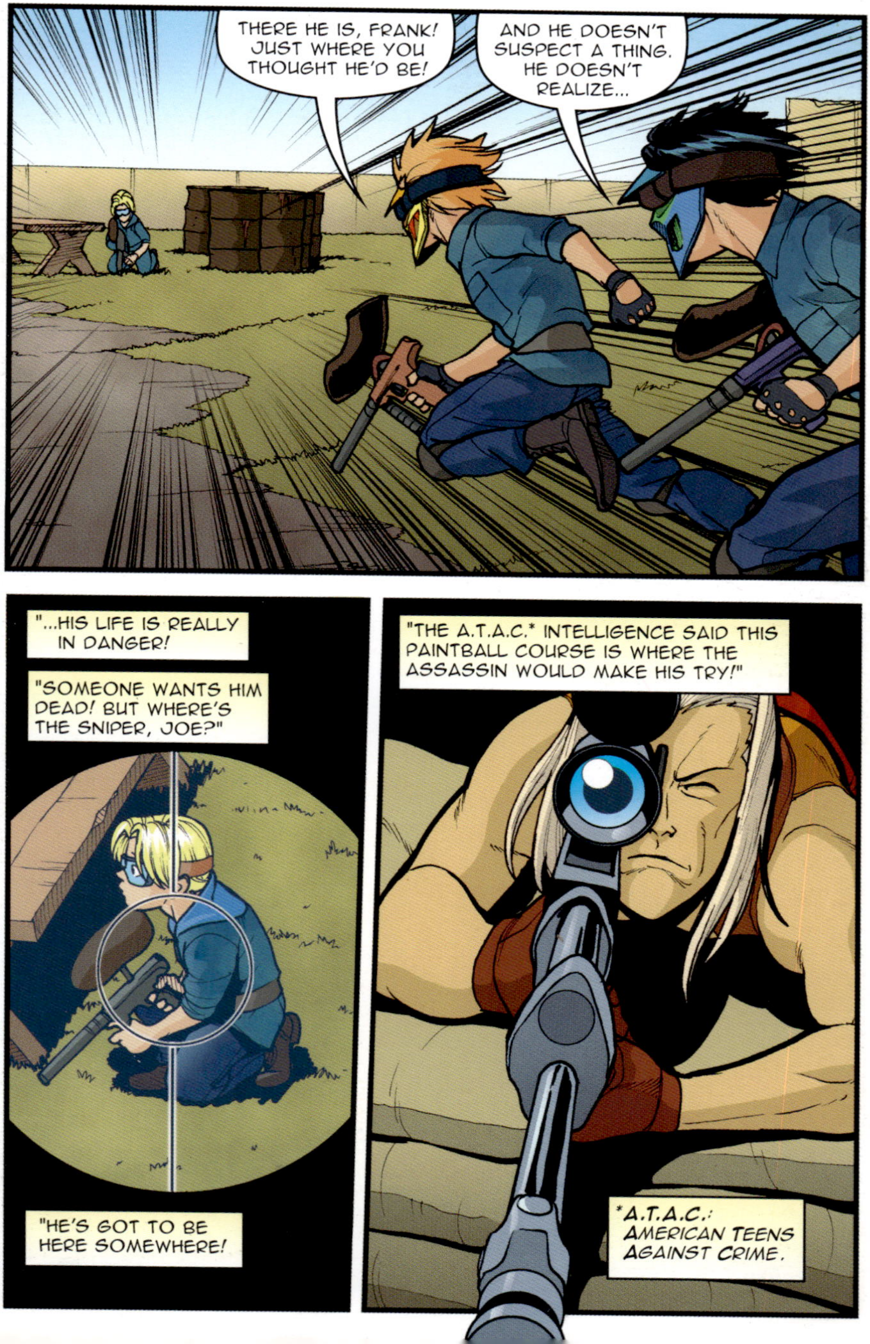
THERE HE IS, FRANK! JUST WHERE YOU THOUGHT HE'D BE!
AND HE DOESN'T SUSPECT A THING. HE DOESN'T REALIZE...
"...HIS LIFE IS REALLY IN DANGER!
"SOMEONE WANTS HIM DEAD! BUT WHERE'S THE SNIPER, JOE?"
"HE'S GOT TO BE HERE SOMEWHERE!
"THE A.T.A.C.* INTELLIGENCE SAID THIS PAINTBALL COURSE IS WHERE THE ASSASSIN WOULD MAKE HIS TRY!"
*A.T.A.C.: AMERICAN TEENS AGAINST CRIME.

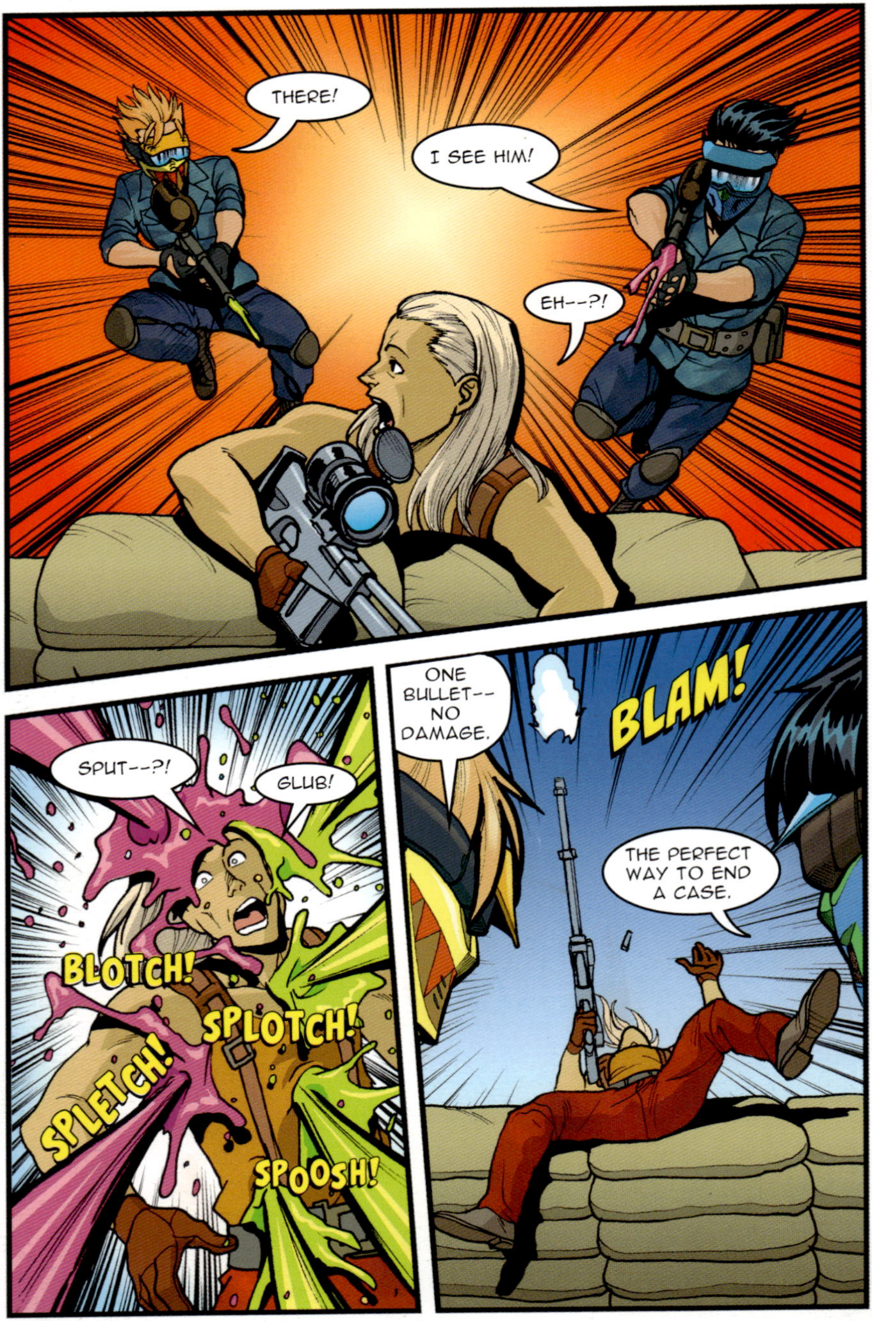
THERE!
I SEE HIM!
EH--?!
SPUT--?!
GLUB!
BLOTCH!
SPLOTCH!
SPLETCH!
SPOOSH!
ONE BULLET-- NO DAMAGE.
BLAM!
THE PERFECT WAY TO END A CASE.

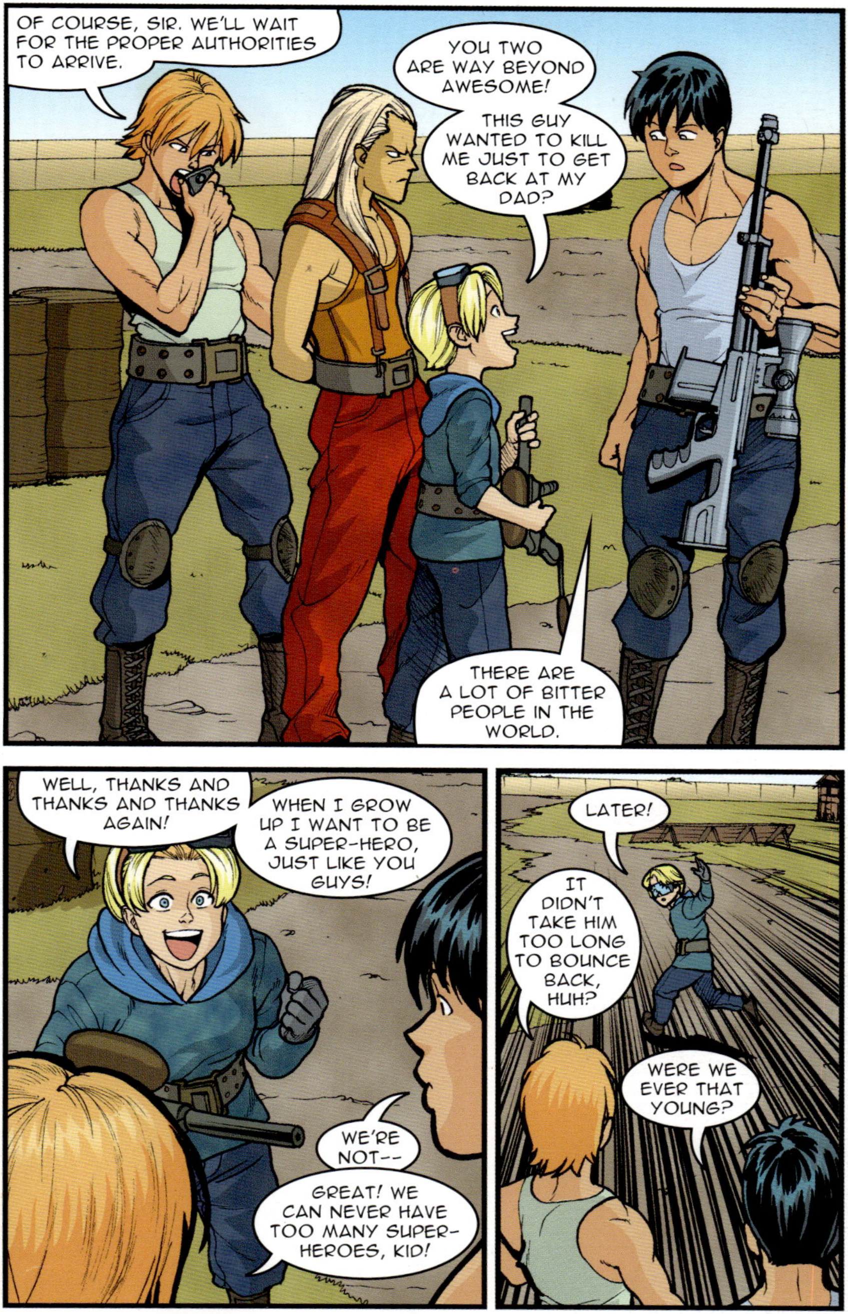
OF COURSE, SIR. WE'LL WAIT FOR THE PROPER AUTHORITIES TO ARRIVE.
YOU TWO ARE WAY BEYOND AWESOME!
THIS GUY WANTED TO KILL ME JUST TO GET BACK AT MY DAD?
THERE ARE A LOT OF BITTER PEOPLE IN THE WORLD.
WELL, THANKS AND THANKS AND THANKS AGAIN!
WHEN I GROW UP I WANT TO BE A SUPER-HERO, JUST LIKE YOU GUYS!
WE'RE NOT--
GREAT! WE CAN NEVER HAVE TOO MANY SUPER-HEROES, KID!
LATER!
IT DIDN'T TAKE HIM TOO LONG TO BOUNCE BACK, HUH?
WERE WE EVER THAT YOUNG?

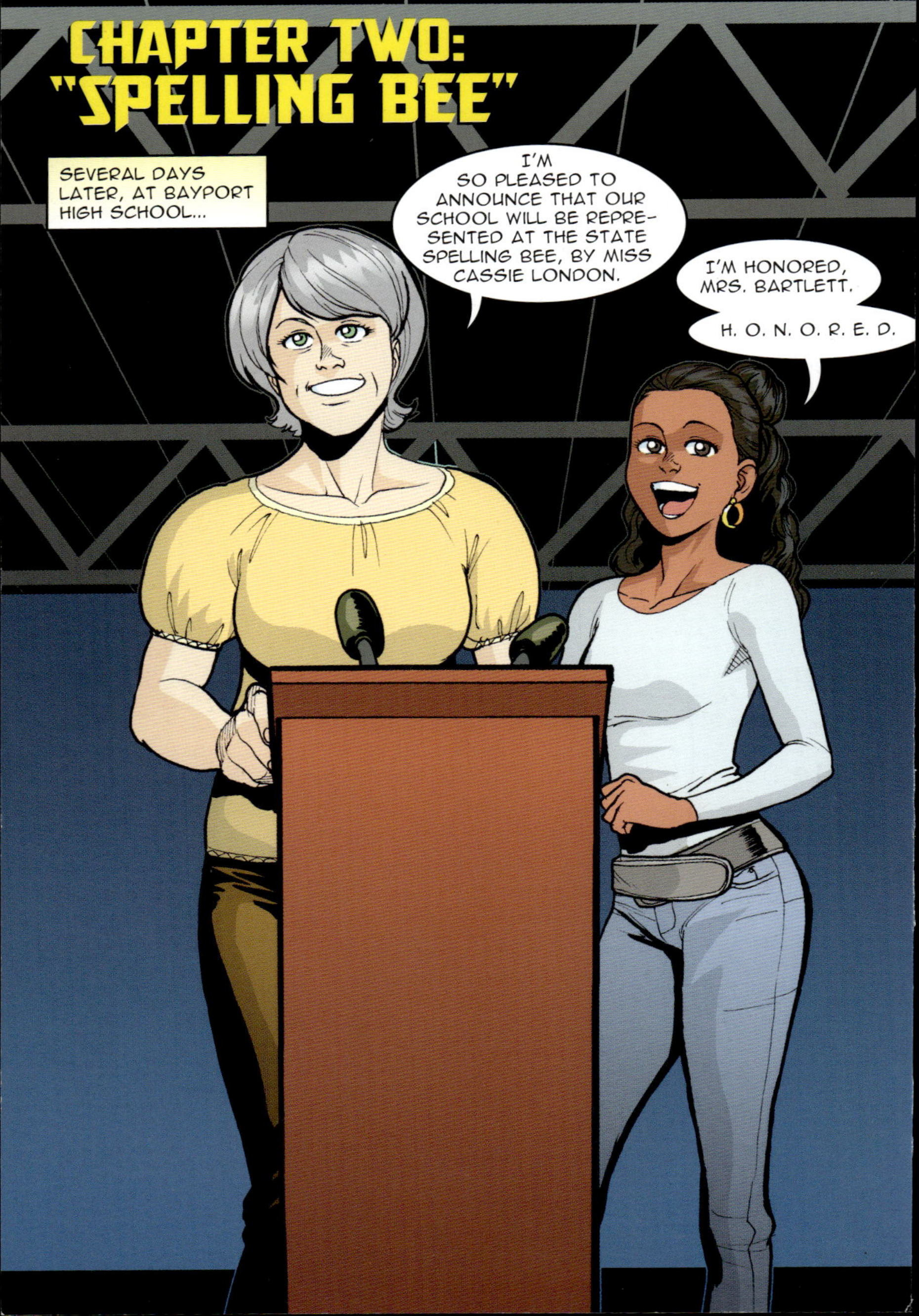
CHAPTER TWO:
"SPELLING BEE"
SEVERAL DAYS LATER, AT BAYPORT HIGH SCHOOL...
I'M SO PLEASED TO ANNOUNCE THAT OUR SCHOOL WILL BE REPRESENTED AT THE STATE SPELLING BEE, BY MISS CASSIE LONDON.
I'M HONORED, MRS. BARTLETT.
H. O. N. O. R. E. D.

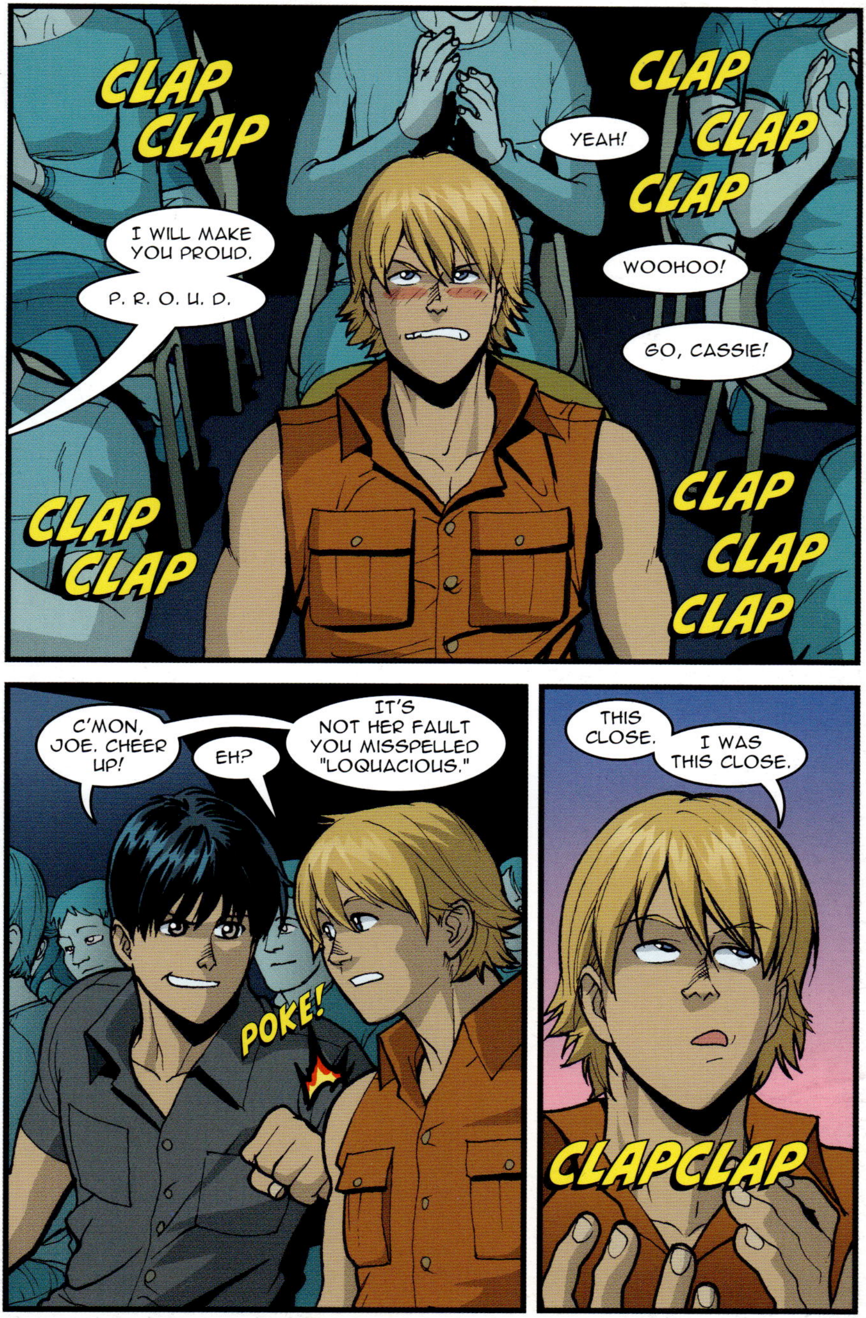
CLAP
CLAP
CLAP
CLAP
CLAP
YEAH!
I WILL MAKE YOU PROUD.
P. R. O. U. D.
WOOHOO!
GO, CASSIE!
CLAP
CLAP
CLAP
CLAP
CLAP
C'MON, JOE. CHEER UP!
EH?
IT'S NOT HER FAULT YOU MISSPELLED "LOQUACIOUS."
POKE!
THIS CLOSE.
I WAS THIS CLOSE.
CLAPCLAP

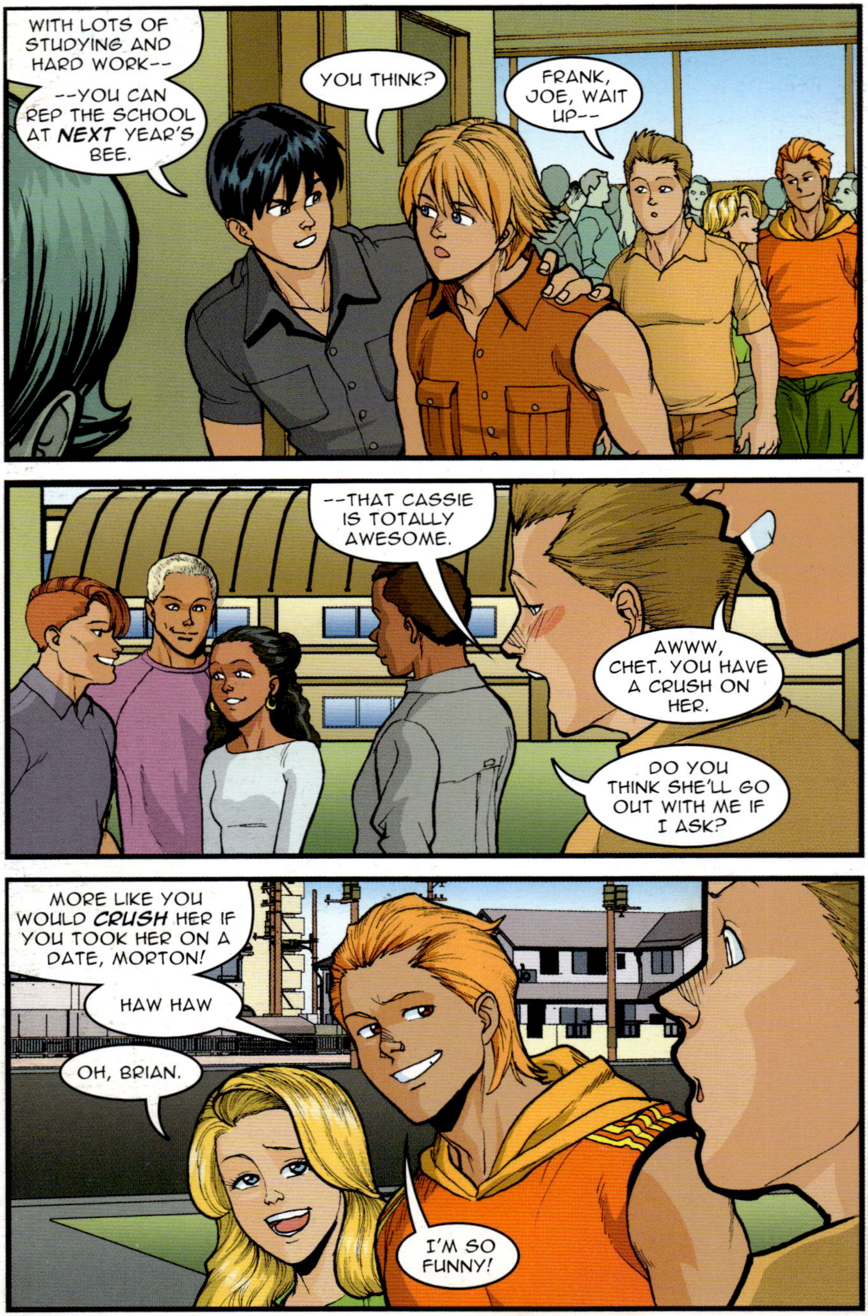
WITH LOTS OF STUDYING AND HARD WORK--
--YOU CAN REP THE SCHOOL AT ***NEXT*** YEAR'S BEE.
YOU THINK?
FRANK, JOE, WAIT UP--
--THAT CASSIE IS TOTALLY AWESOME.
AWWW, CHET. YOU HAVE A CRUSH ON HER.
DO YOU THINK SHE'LL GO OUT WITH ME IF I ASK?
MORE LIKE YOU WOULD ***CRUSH*** HER IF YOU TOOK HER ON A DATE, MORTON!
HAW HAW
OH, BRIAN.
I'M SO FUNNY!

IF SHE DEIGNED TO DATE YOU IT WOULD BE FOR AN ANTHROPOLOGICAL RESEARCH PROJECT.
RIGHT?
GOOD ONE!
HA HA HEH
WHAT-EV!
WHAT IS "DEIGNED"?
I DON'T KNOW. WHAT IS "ANTHRO-POLOGICAL"?!
HAVE YOU THOUGHT ABOUT SENDING HER FLOWERS?
REALLY? DOES ANYONE DO THAT ANY MORE?
IT'S ALWAYS WORKED FOR ME. WOMEN OF ALL AGES LOVE RHODODENDRONS.
R.H.O.D.O. D.E.N.D.R.O.N.S.

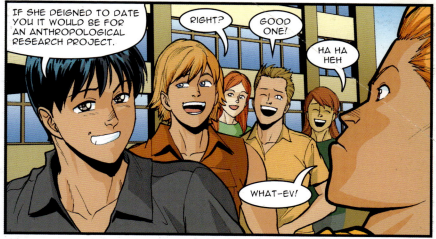

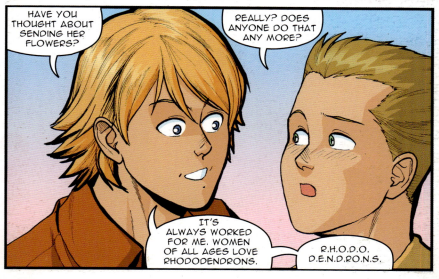

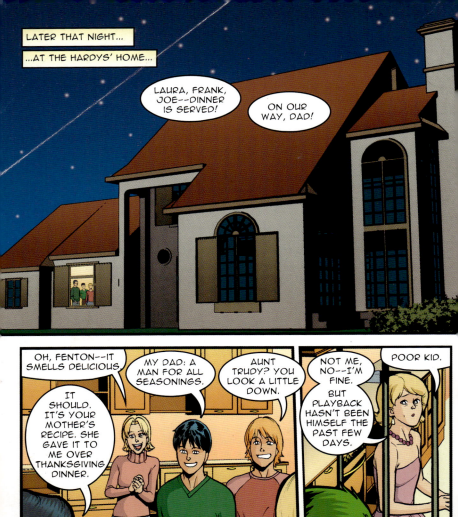

LATER THAT NIGHT...

...AT THE HARDYS' HOME...

LAURA, FRANK, JOE--DINNER IS SERVED!

ON OUR WAY, DAD!

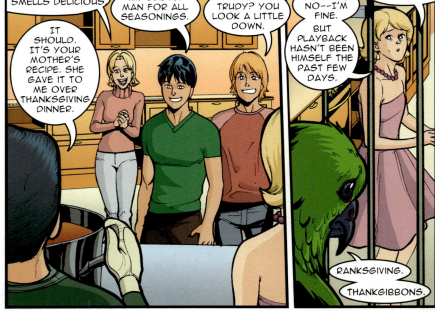

OH, FENTON--IT SMELLS DELICIOUS.

IT SHOULD. IT'S YOUR MOTHER'S RECIPE. SHE GAVE IT TO ME OVER THANKSGIVING DINNER.

MY DAD: A MAN FOR ALL SEASONINGS.

AUNT TRUDY? YOU LOOK A LITTLE DOWN.

NOT ME, NO--I'M FINE.

BUT PLAYBACK HASN'T BEEN HIMSELF THE PAST FEW DAYS.

POOR KID.

RANKSGIVING.

THANKGIBBONS.

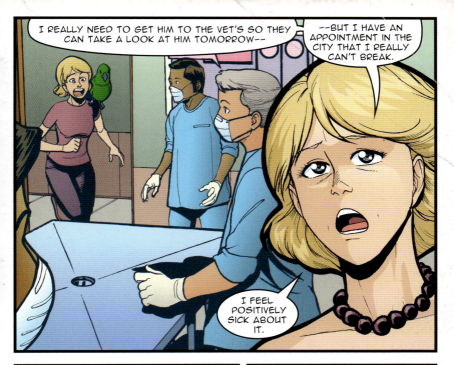

I REALLY NEED TO GET HIM TO THE VET'S SO THEY CAN TAKE A LOOK AT HIM TOMORROW--

--BUT I HAVE AN APPOINTMENT IN THE CITY THAT I REALLY CAN'T BREAK.

I FEEL POSITIVELY SICK ABOUT IT.

DON'T BE SILLY, AUNT TRUDY. WE'RE OFF OF SCHOOL TOMORROW--

--AND I KNOW SOMEONE WHO WOULD LOVE TO SPEND SOME QUALITY TIME WITH A SICK FRIEND.

FRANK WILL TAKE PLAYBACK FOR A CHECK-UP. RIGHT, FRANK?

UH.... SURE. CAN'T THINK OF ANY PLACE ELSE I'D RATHER BE.

OH, FRANK-- THAT'S SO THOUGHTFUL!

I COULD JUST HUG YOU!

UM... YOU ARE HUGGING ME.

TIGHTLY!

HUGFUL... HUGFUL!

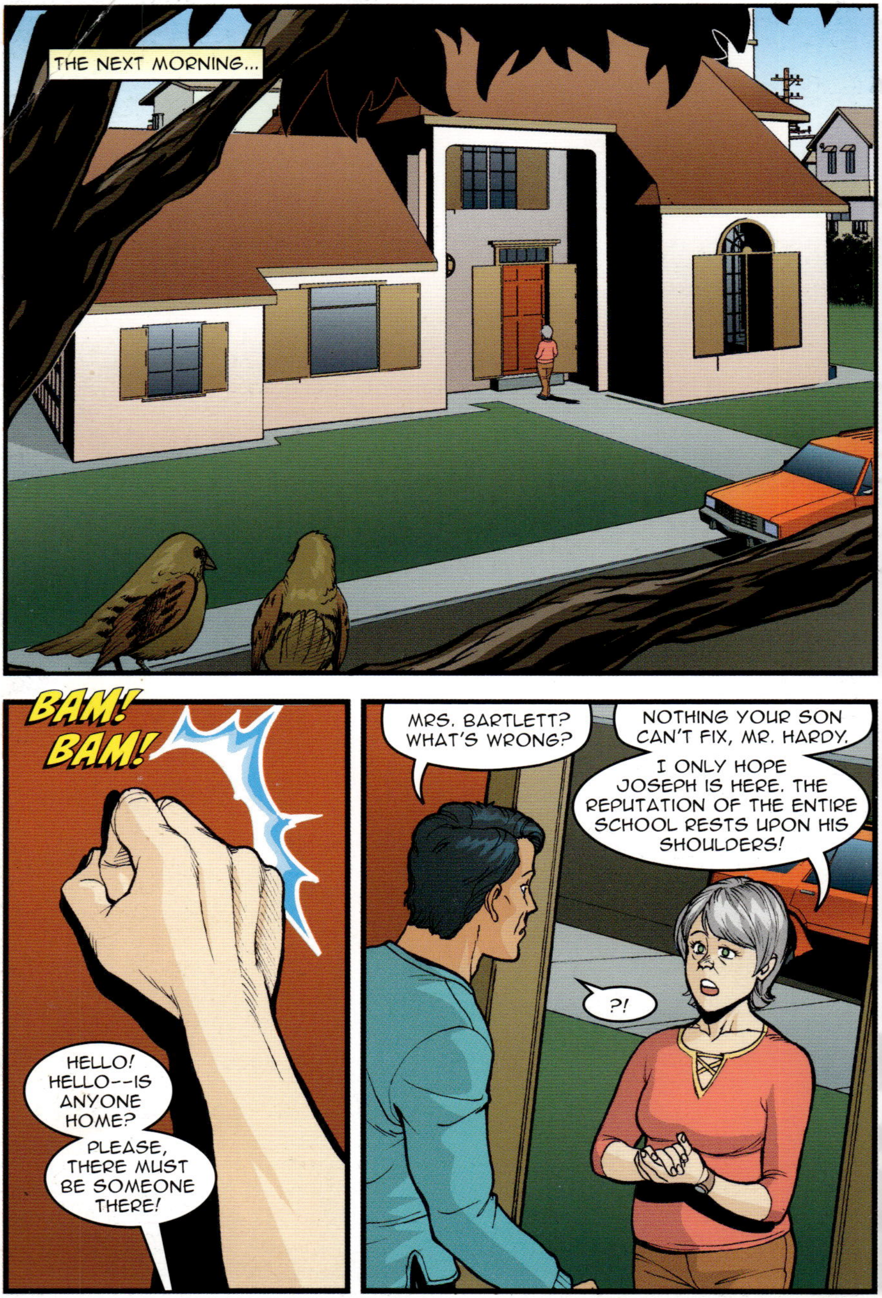
THE NEXT MORNING...
BAM! BAM!
HELLO! HELLO--IS ANYONE HOME?
PLEASE, THERE MUST BE SOMEONE THERE!
MRS. BARTLETT? WHAT'S WRONG?
?!
NOTHING YOUR SON CAN'T FIX, MR. HARDY.
I ONLY HOPE JOSEPH IS HERE. THE REPUTATION OF THE ENTIRE SCHOOL RESTS UPON HIS SHOULDERS!

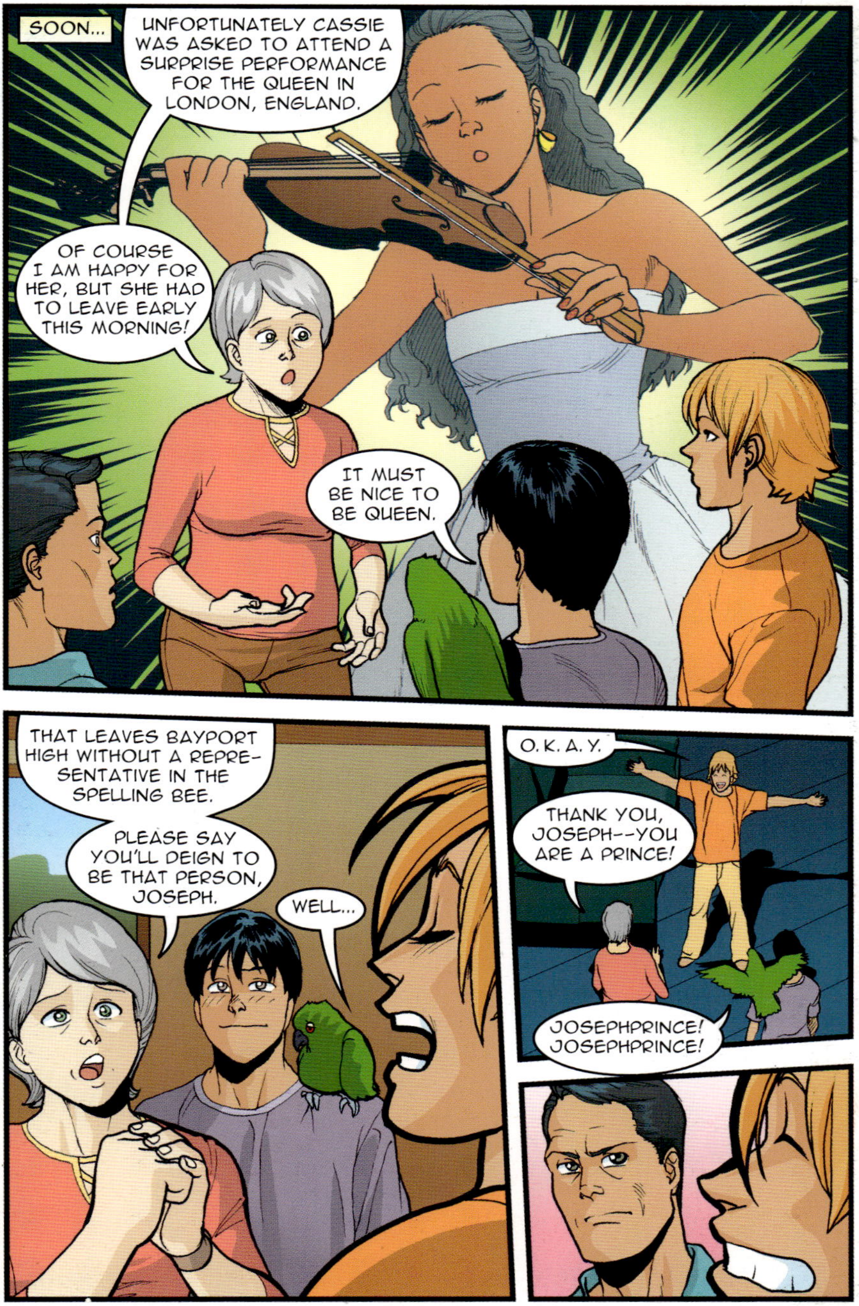
SOON...
UNFORTUNATELY CASSIE WAS ASKED TO ATTEND A SURPRISE PERFORMANCE FOR THE QUEEN IN LONDON, ENGLAND.
OF COURSE I AM HAPPY FOR HER, BUT SHE HAD TO LEAVE EARLY THIS MORNING!
IT MUST BE NICE TO BE QUEEN.
THAT LEAVES BAYPORT HIGH WITHOUT A REPRE-SENTATIVE IN THE SPELLING BEE.
PLEASE SAY YOU'LL DEIGN TO BE THAT PERSON, JOSEPH.
WELL...
O. K. A. Y.
THANK YOU, JOSEPH--YOU ARE A PRINCE!
JOSEPHPRINCE! JOSEPHPRINCE!

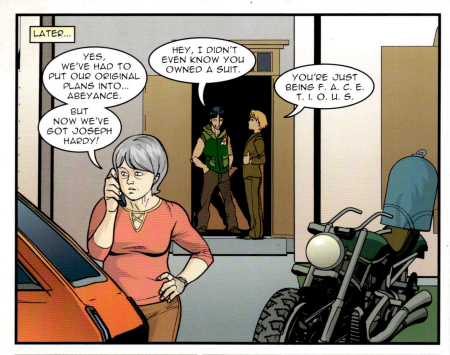

LATER...

YES, WE'VE HAD TO PUT OUR ORIGINAL PLANS INTO... ABEYANCE.

BUT NOW WE'VE GOT JOSEPH HARDY!

HEY, I DIDN'T EVEN KNOW YOU OWNED A SUIT.

YOU'RE JUST BEING F. A. C. E. T. I. O. U. S.

OH... AND GOOD LUCK.

VRMMM

LOOKS LIKE IT'S JUST ME AND YOU, PLAYBACK.

DON'T WORRY-- YOU'RE GOING TO BE FINE.

BAY OUNCE.

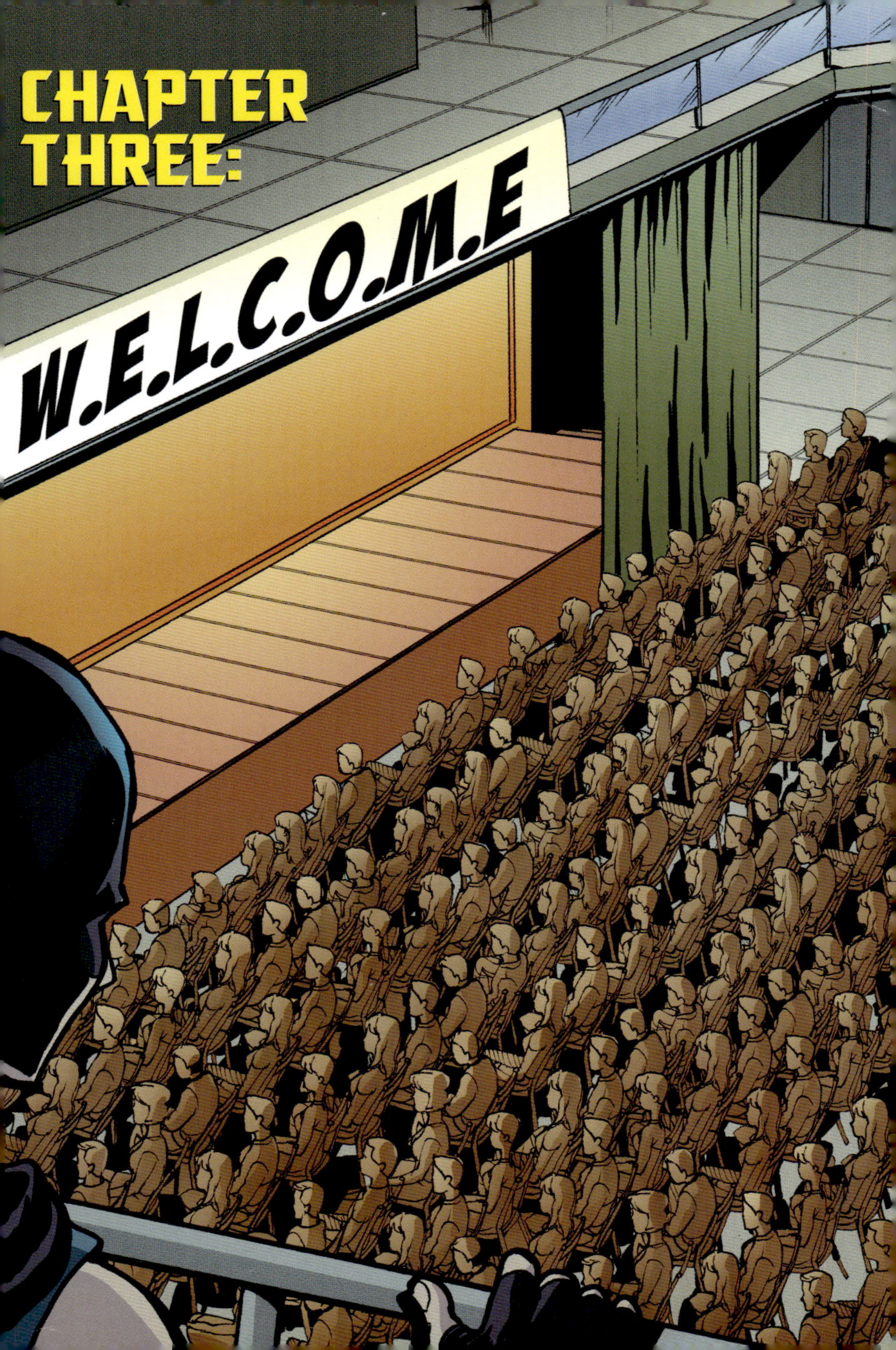
CHAPTER THREE:
W.E.L.C.O.M.E

I'VE SOLVED MURDERS, FOUGHT TERRORISTS, RESCUED KIDNAPPED KIDS...

... SO WHY IS A SPELLING BEE GETTING ME ANXIOUS?

HELLO.

HI BACK.

KEEP YOUR HEAD IN THE GAME, JOE.

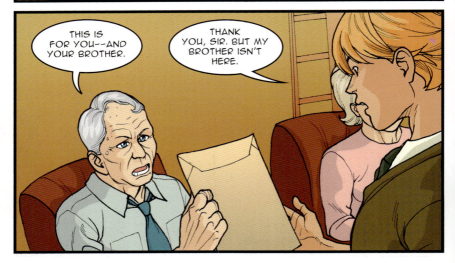

THIS IS FOR YOU--AND YOUR BROTHER.

THANK YOU, SIR. BUT MY BROTHER ISN'T HERE.

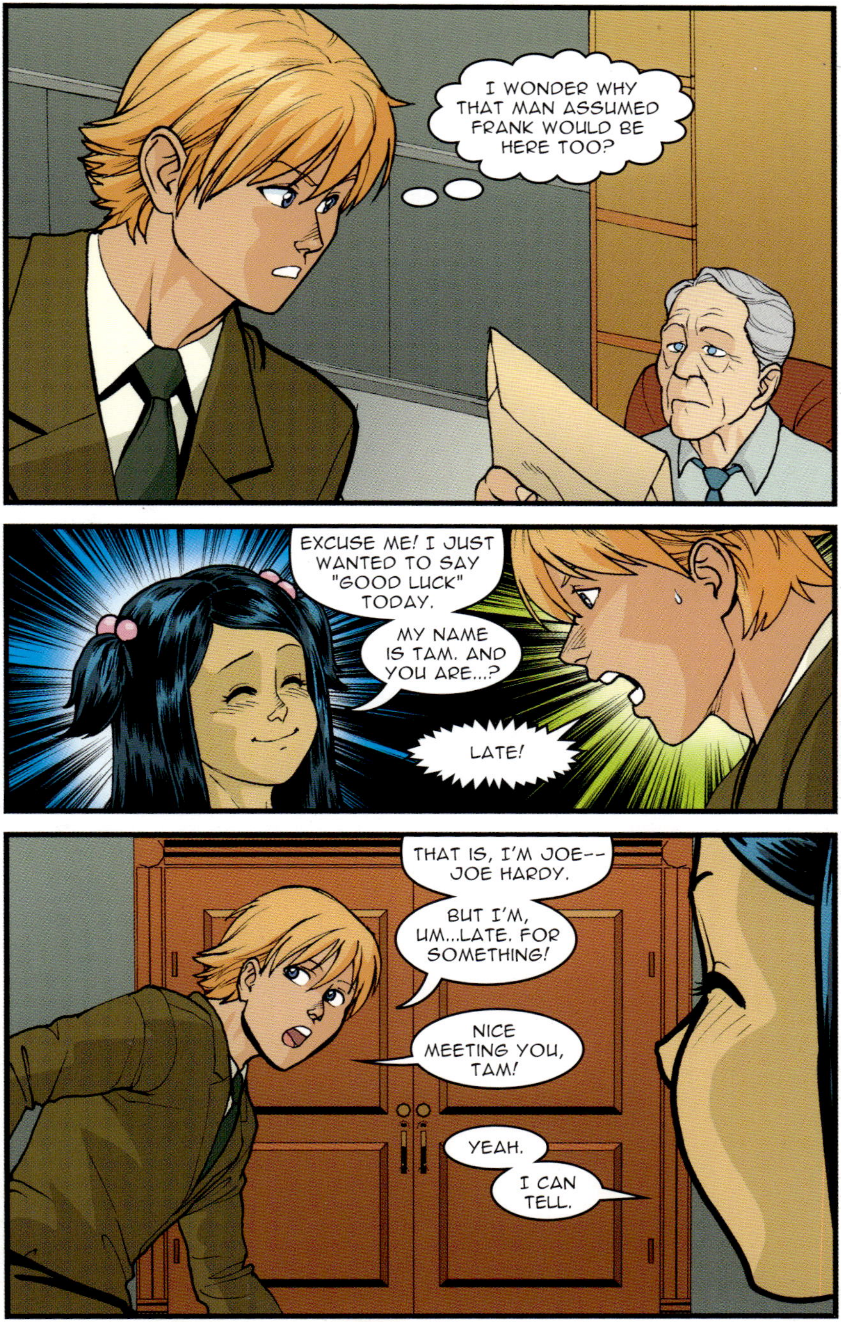
I WONDER WHY THAT MAN ASSUMED FRANK WOULD BE HERE TOO?
EXCUSE ME! I JUST WANTED TO SAY "GOOD LUCK" TODAY.
MY NAME IS TAM. AND YOU ARE...?
LATE!
THAT IS, I'M JOE-- JOE HARDY.
BUT I'M, UM...LATE. FOR SOMETHING!
NICE MEETING YOU, TAM!
YEAH.
I CAN TELL.

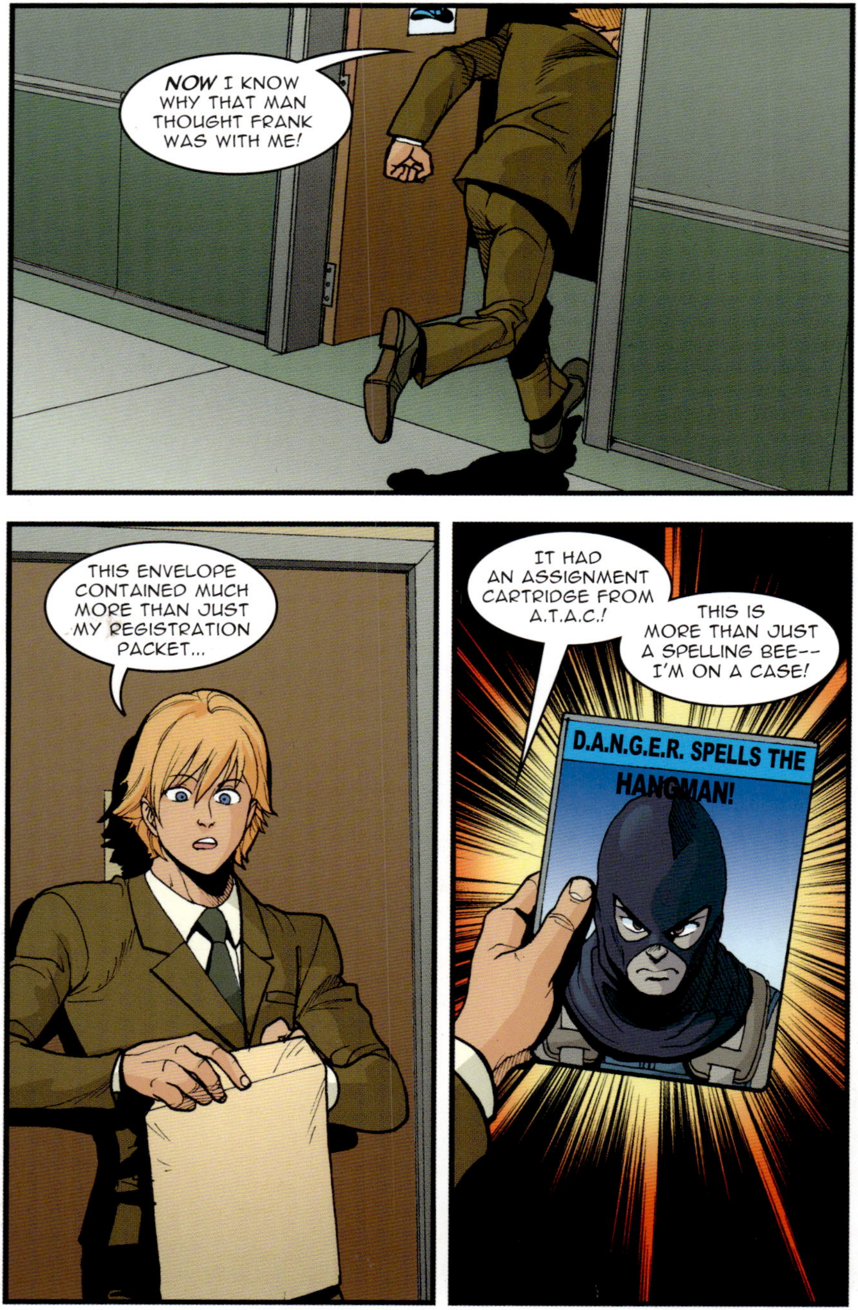
NOW I KNOW WHY THAT MAN THOUGHT FRANK WAS WITH ME!
THIS ENVELOPE CONTAINED MUCH MORE THAN JUST MY REGISTRATION PACKET...
IT HAD AN ASSIGNMENT CARTRIDGE FROM A.T.A.C.!
THIS IS MORE THAN JUST A SPELLING BEE-- I'M ON A CASE!
D.A.N.G.E.R. SPELLS THE HANGMAN!

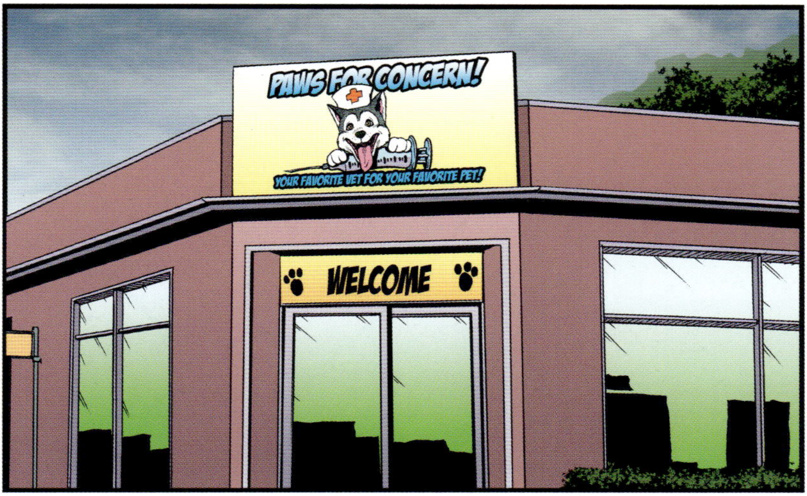
PAWS FOR CONCERN!
YOUR FAVORITE VET FOR YOUR FAVORITE PET!
WELCOME

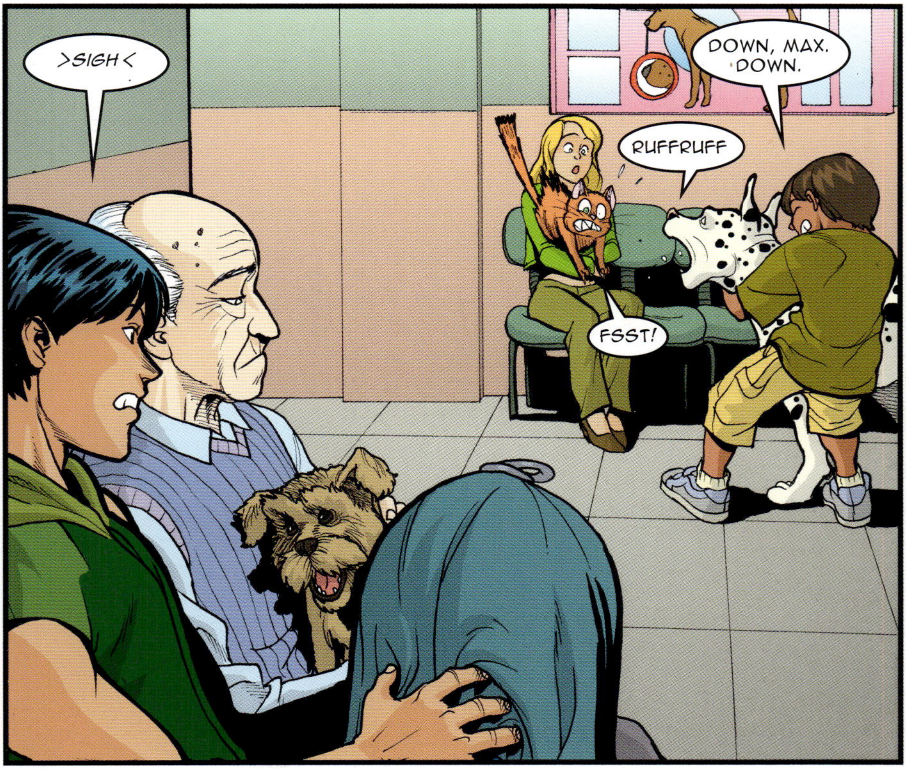
>SIGH<
DOWN, MAX. DOWN.
RUFFRUFF
FSST!

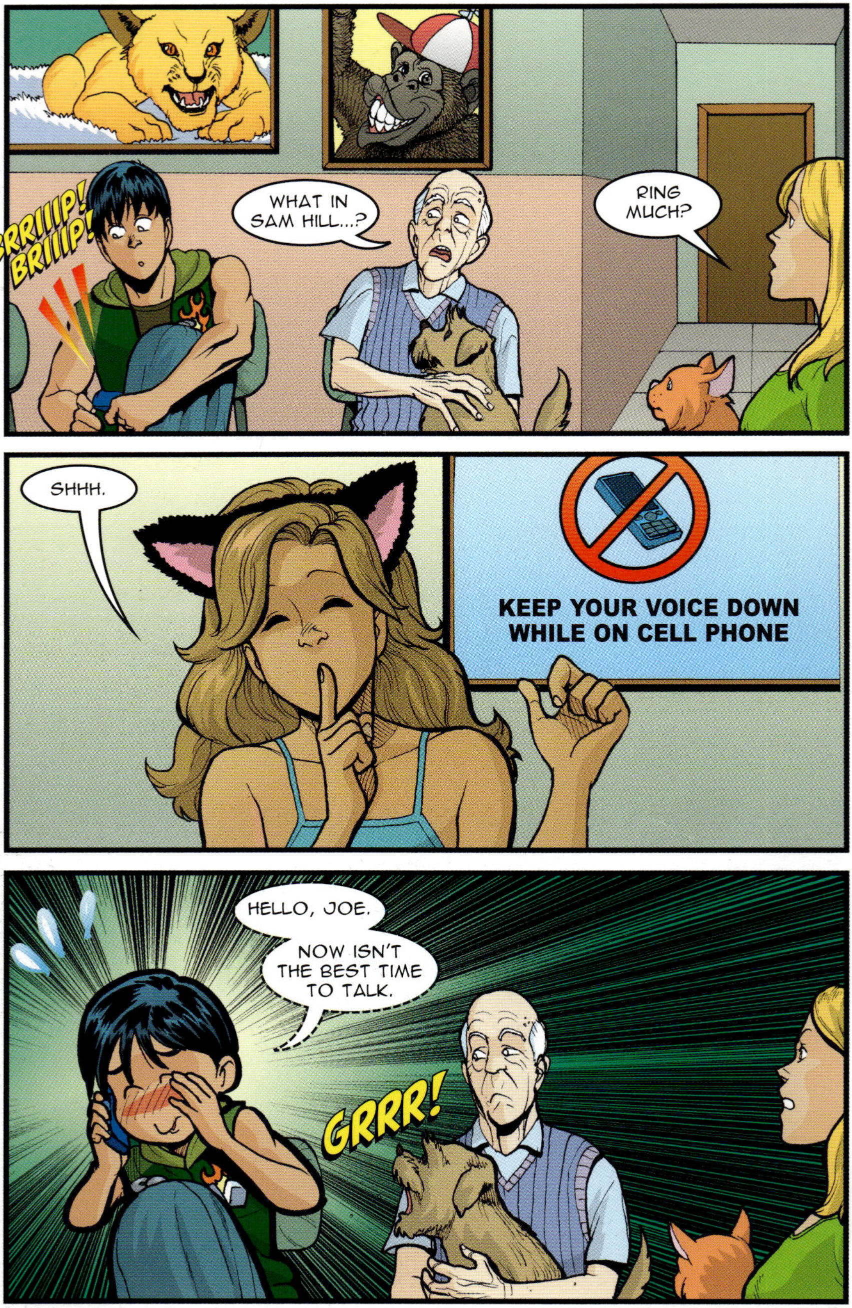
BRRIIIP! BRIIIP!
WHAT IN SAM HILL...?
RING MUCH?
SHHH.
KEEP YOUR VOICE DOWN WHILE ON CELL PHONE
HELLO, JOE.
NOW ISN'T THE BEST TIME TO TALK.
GRRR!

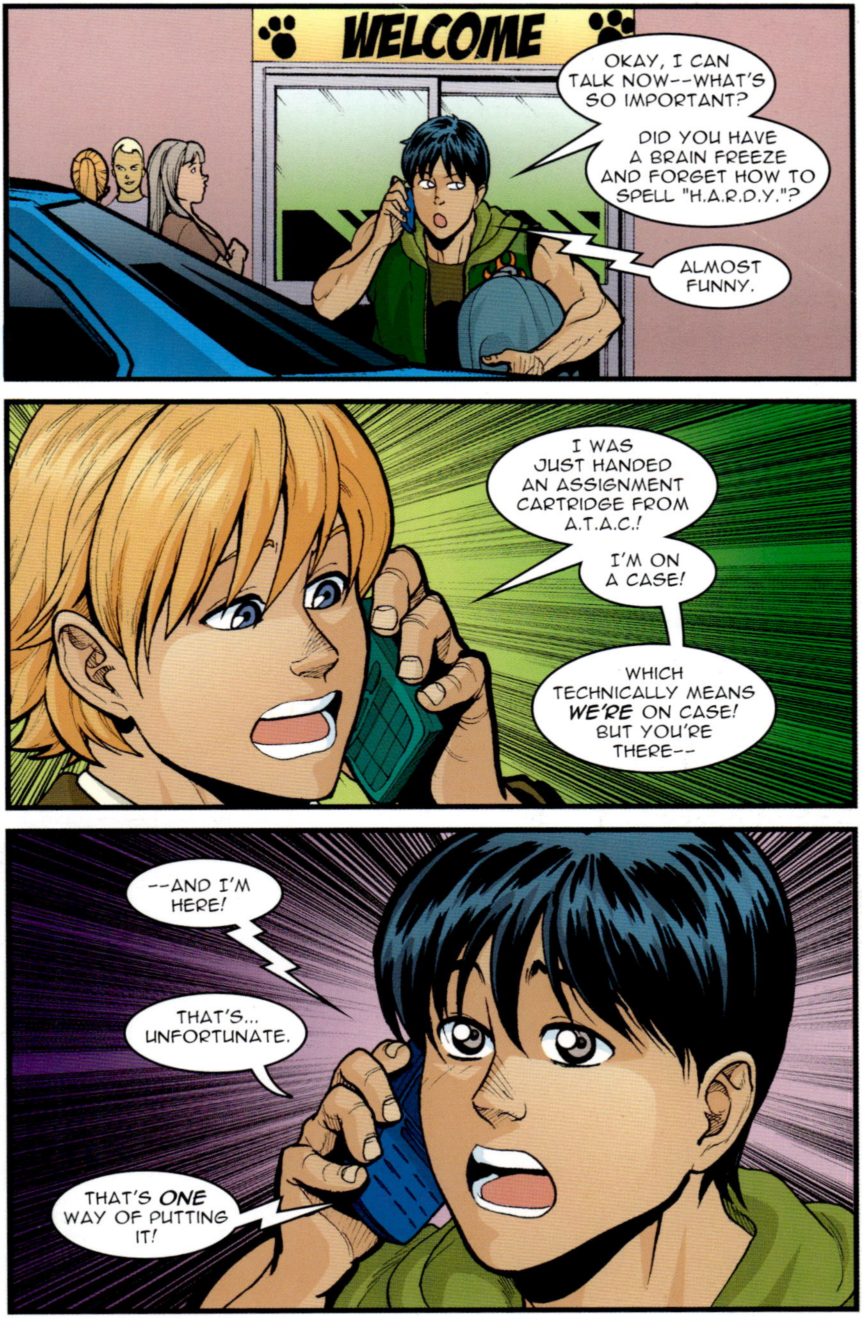
WELCOME
OKAY, I CAN TALK NOW--WHAT'S SO IMPORTANT?
DID YOU HAVE A BRAIN FREEZE AND FORGET HOW TO SPELL "H.A.R.D.Y."?
ALMOST FUNNY.
I WAS JUST HANDED AN ASSIGNMENT CARTRIDGE FROM A.T.A.C.!
I'M ON A CASE!
WHICH TECHNICALLY MEANS *WE'RE* ON CASE! BUT YOU'RE THERE--
--AND I'M HERE!
THAT'S... UNFORTUNATE.
THAT'S *ONE* WAY OF PUTTING IT!

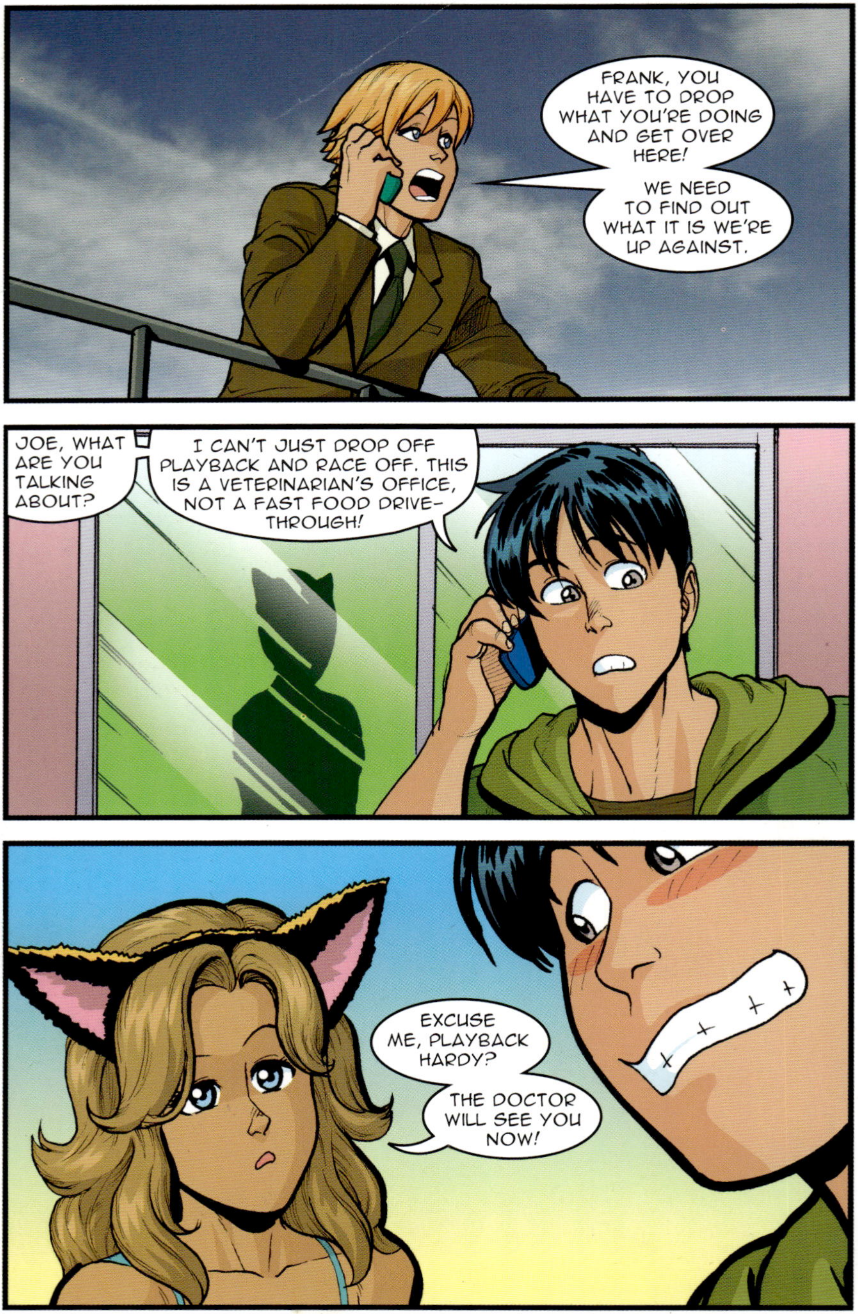
FRANK, YOU HAVE TO DROP WHAT YOU'RE DOING AND GET OVER HERE!
WE NEED TO FIND OUT WHAT IT IS WE'RE UP AGAINST.
JOE, WHAT ARE YOU TALKING ABOUT?
I CAN'T JUST DROP OFF PLAYBACK AND RACE OFF. THIS IS A VETERINARIAN'S OFFICE, NOT A FAST FOOD DRIVE-THROUGH!
EXCUSE ME, PLAYBACK HARDY?
THE DOCTOR WILL SEE YOU NOW!

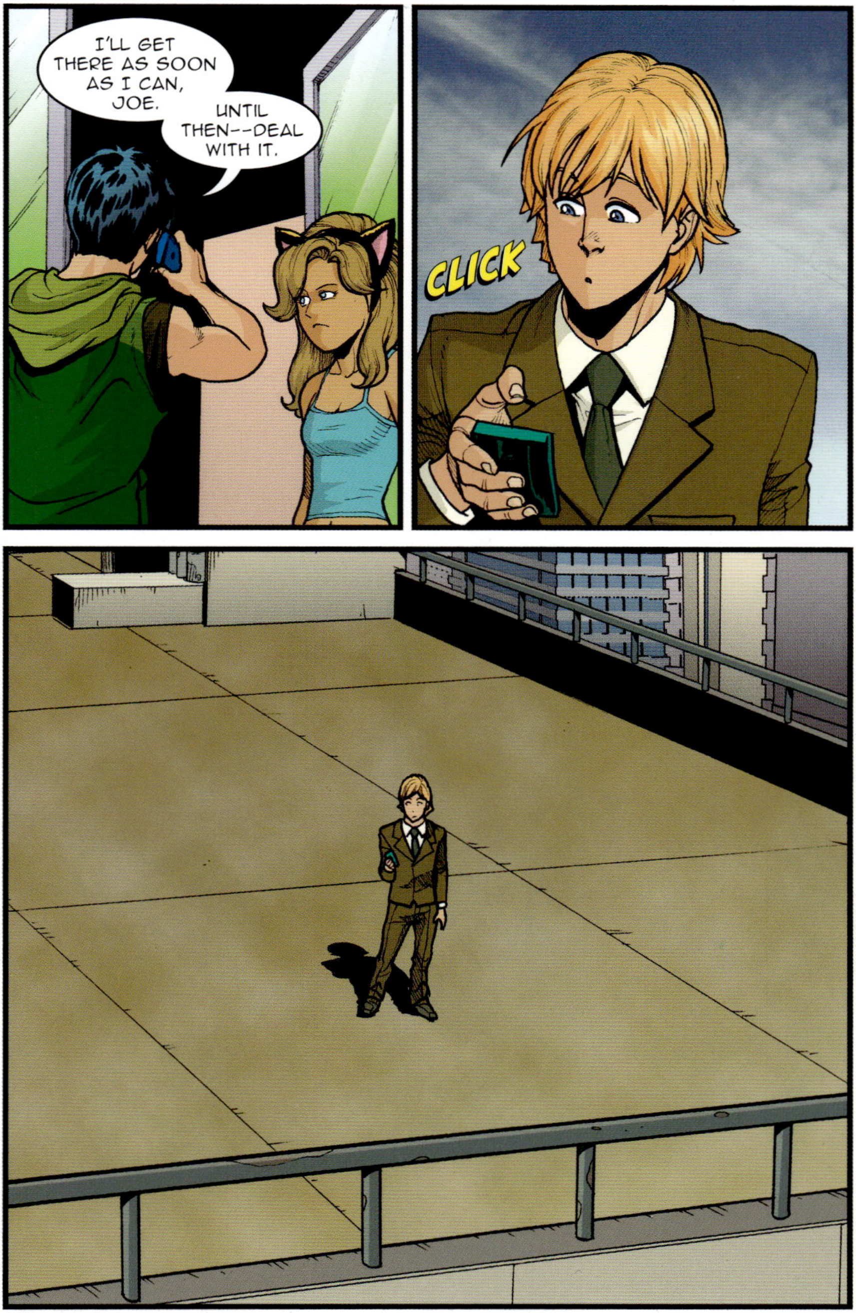
I'LL GET THERE AS SOON AS I CAN, JOE.
UNTIL THEN--DEAL WITH IT.
CLICK

I'M NOT EVEN SURE HOW I'M SUPPOSED TO WATCH THIS THING SO FAR AWAY FROM ANY OF THOSE TECHNO GEEKED-OUT PLAYER CONSOLES.

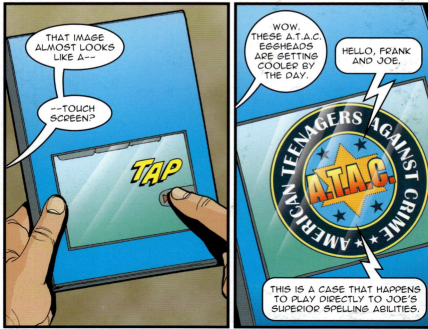

THAT IMAGE ALMOST LOOKS LIKE A--

--TOUCH SCREEN?

TAP

WOW. THESE A.T.A.C. EGGHEADS ARE GETTING COOLER BY THE DAY.

HELLO, FRANK AND JOE.

A.T.A.C.

AMERICAN TEENAGERS AGAINST CRIME

THIS IS A CASE THAT HAPPENS TO PLAY DIRECTLY TO JOE'S SUPERIOR SPELLING ABILITIES.

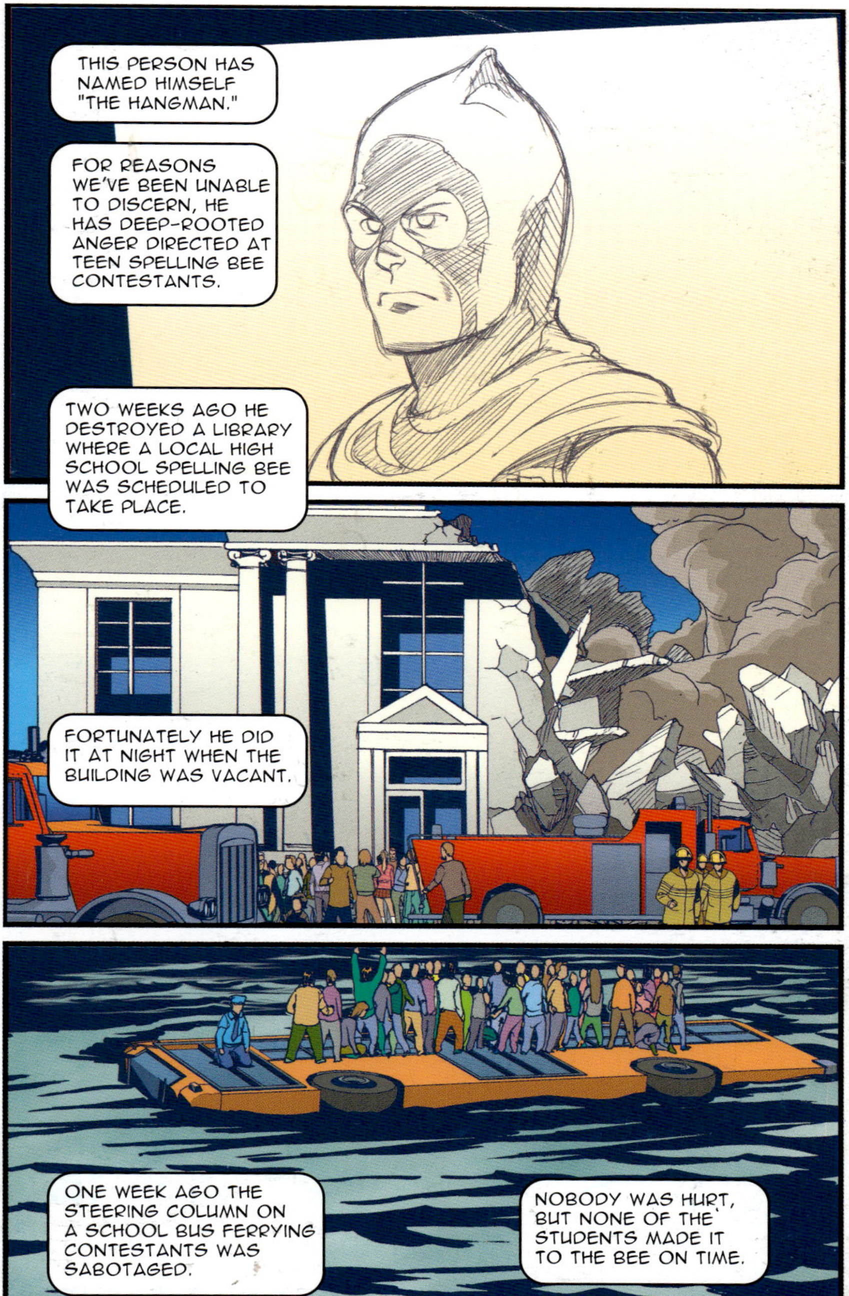
THIS PERSON HAS NAMED HIMSELF "THE HANGMAN."
FOR REASONS WE'VE BEEN UNABLE TO DISCERN, HE HAS DEEP-ROOTED ANGER DIRECTED AT TEEN SPELLING BEE CONTESTANTS.
TWO WEEKS AGO HE DESTROYED A LIBRARY WHERE A LOCAL HIGH SCHOOL SPELLING BEE WAS SCHEDULED TO TAKE PLACE.
FORTUNATELY HE DID IT AT NIGHT WHEN THE BUILDING WAS VACANT.
ONE WEEK AGO THE STEERING COLUMN ON A SCHOOL BUS FERRYING CONTESTANTS WAS SABOTAGED.
NOBODY WAS HURT, BUT NONE OF THE STUDENTS MADE IT TO THE BEE ON TIME.

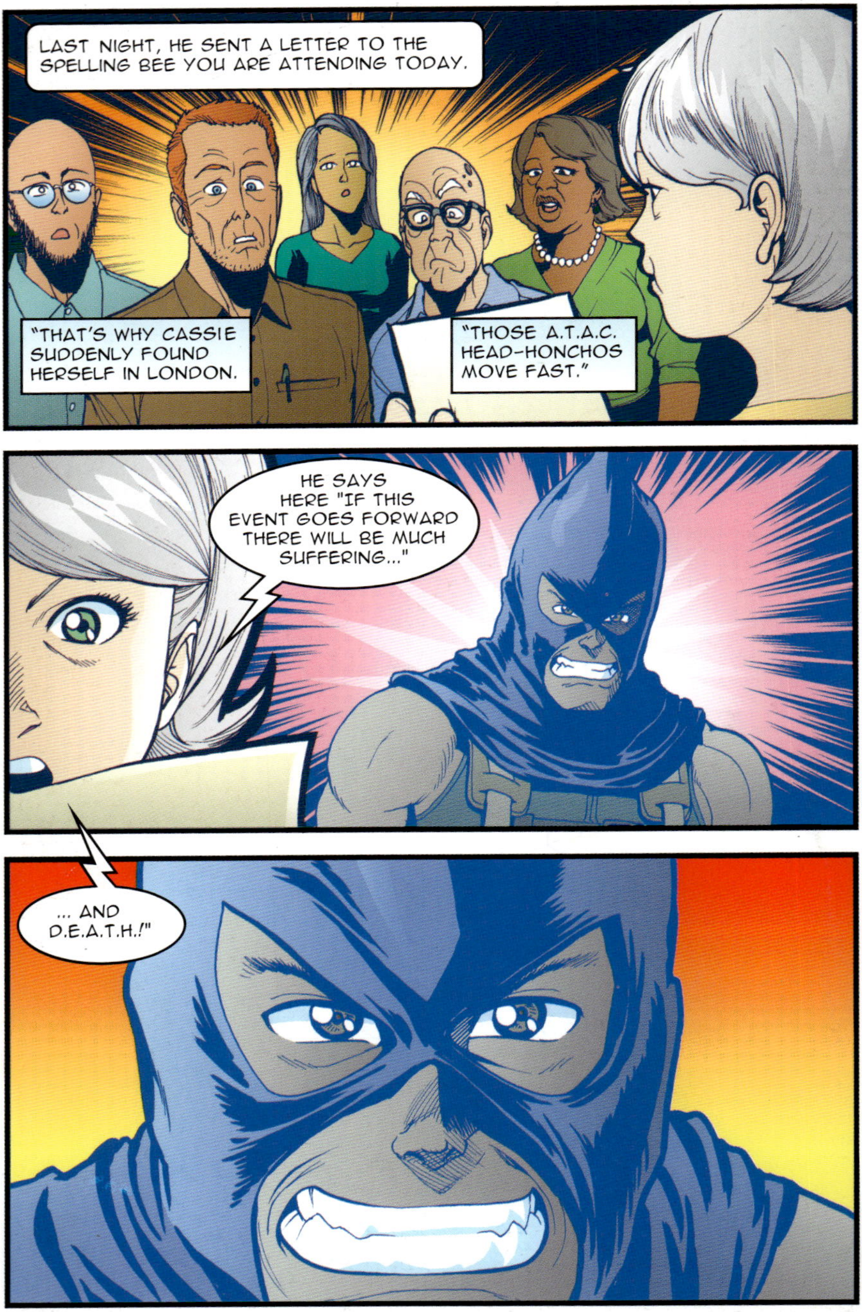
LAST NIGHT, HE SENT A LETTER TO THE SPELLING BEE YOU ARE ATTENDING TODAY.
"THAT'S WHY CASSIE SUDDENLY FOUND HERSELF IN LONDON.
"THOSE A.T.A.C. HEAD-HONCHOS MOVE FAST."
HE SAYS HERE "IF THIS EVENT GOES FORWARD THERE WILL BE MUCH SUFFERING..."
... AND D.E.A.T.H.!"

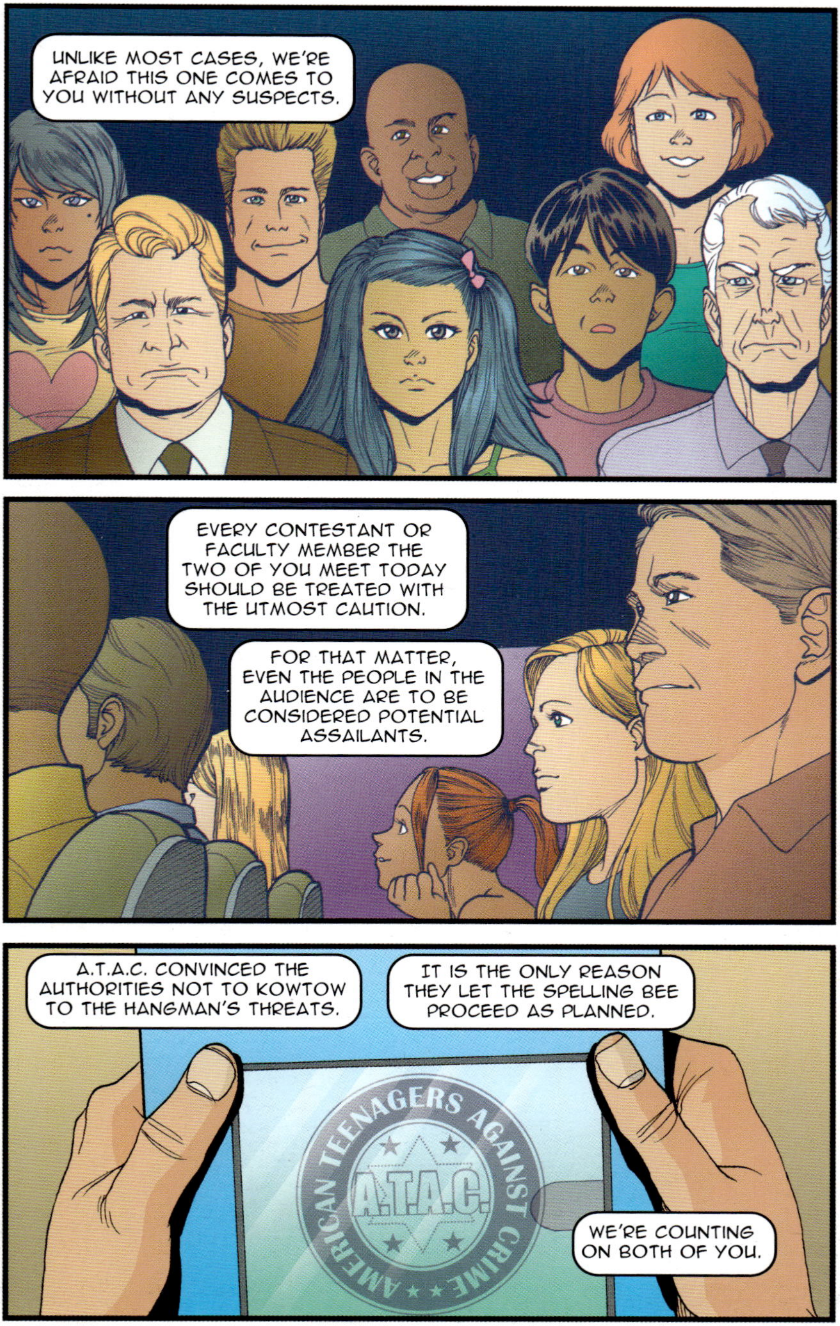
UNLIKE MOST CASES, WE'RE AFRAID THIS ONE COMES TO YOU WITHOUT ANY SUSPECTS.
EVERY CONTESTANT OR FACULTY MEMBER THE TWO OF YOU MEET TODAY SHOULD BE TREATED WITH THE UTMOST CAUTION.
FOR THAT MATTER, EVEN THE PEOPLE IN THE AUDIENCE ARE TO BE CONSIDERED POTENTIAL ASSAILANTS.
A.T.A.C. CONVINCED THE AUTHORITIES NOT TO KOWTOW TO THE HANGMAN'S THREATS.
IT IS THE ONLY REASON THEY LET THE SPELLING BEE PROCEED AS PLANNED.
AMERICAN TEENAGERS AGAINST CRIME
A.T.A.C.
WE'RE COUNTING ON BOTH OF YOU.

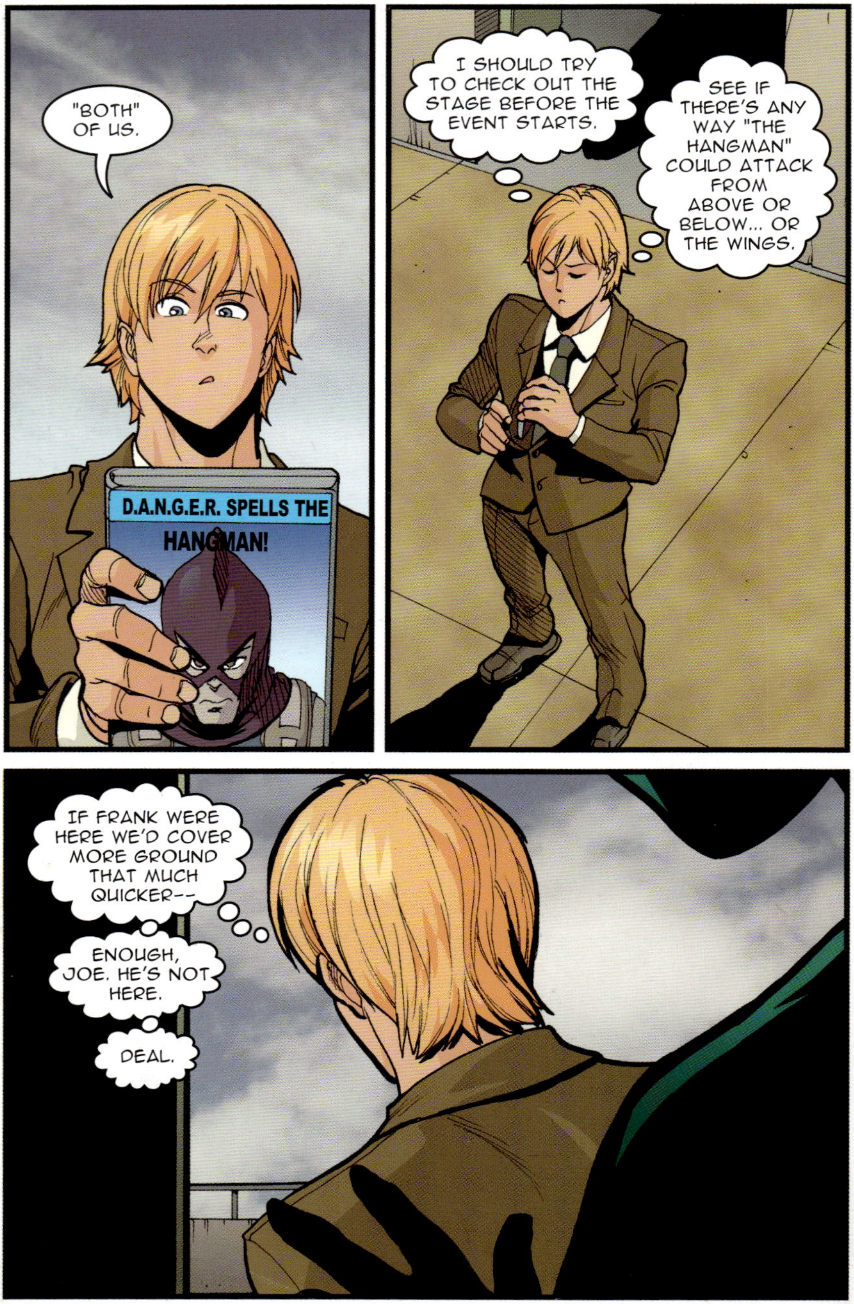
"BOTH" OF US.
D.A.N.G.E.R. SPELLS THE HANGMAN!
I SHOULD TRY TO CHECK OUT THE STAGE BEFORE THE EVENT STARTS.
SEE IF THERE'S ANY WAY "THE HANGMAN" COULD ATTACK FROM ABOVE OR BELOW... OR THE WINGS.
IF FRANK WERE HERE WE'D COVER MORE GROUND THAT MUCH QUICKER--
ENOUGH, JOE. HE'S NOT HERE.
DEAL.

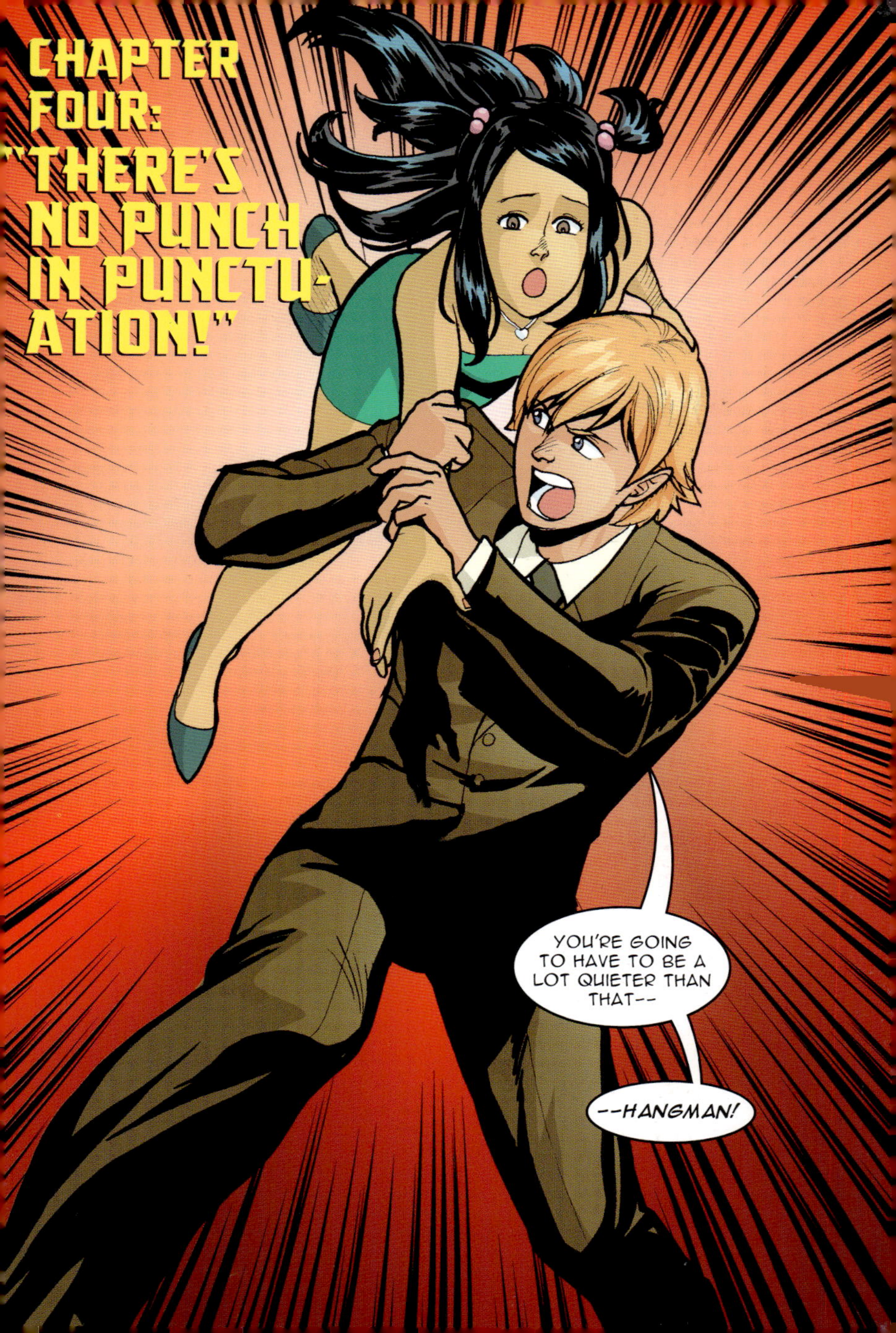
CHAPTER FOUR: "THERE'S NO PUNCH IN PUNCTU-ATION!"
YOU'RE GOING TO HAVE TO BE A LOT QUIETER THAN THAT--
--HANGMAN!

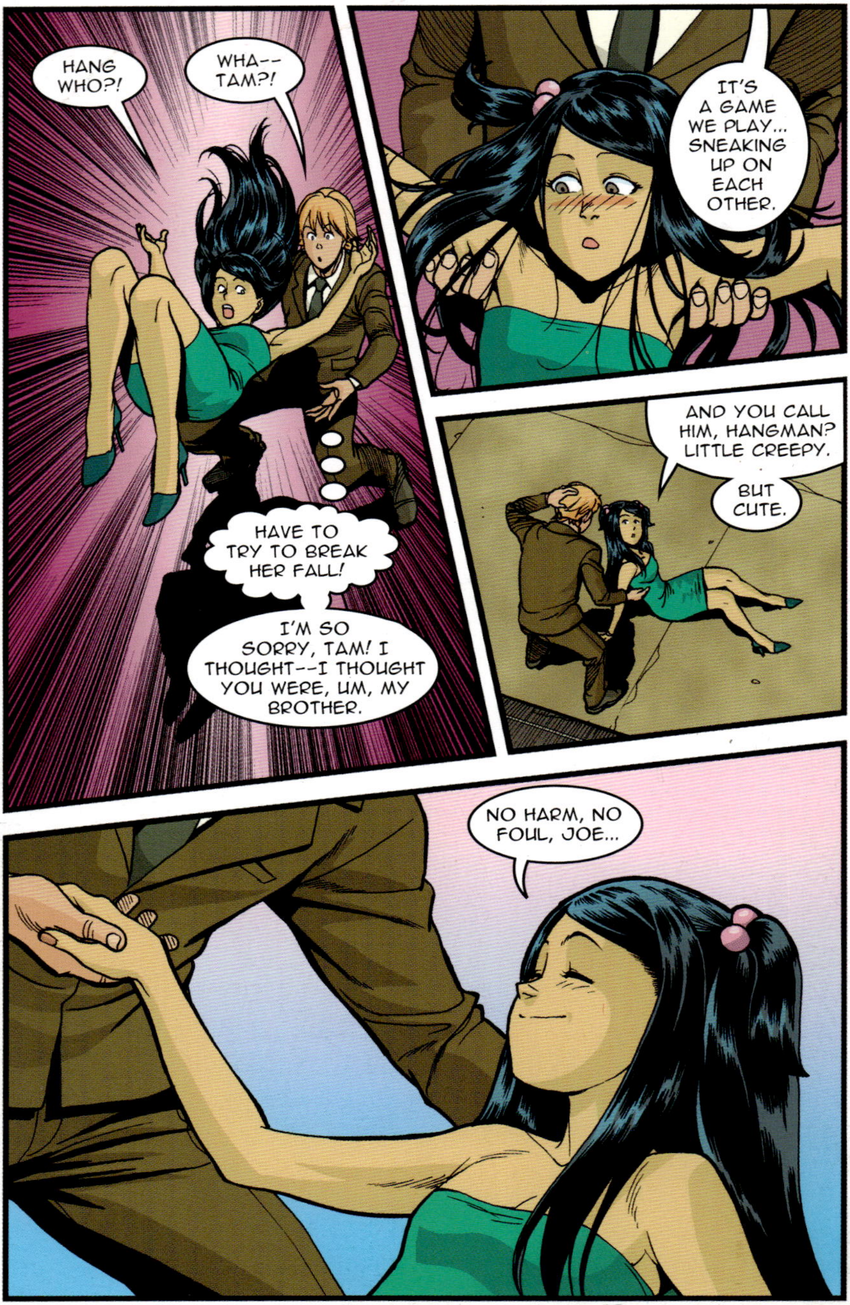
HANG WHO?!
WHA-- TAM?!
HAVE TO TRY TO BREAK HER FALL!
I'M SO SORRY, TAM! I THOUGHT--I THOUGHT YOU WERE, UM, MY BROTHER.
IT'S A GAME WE PLAY... SNEAKING UP ON EACH OTHER.
AND YOU CALL HIM, HANGMAN? LITTLE CREEPY.
BUT CUTE.
NO HARM, NO FOUL, JOE...

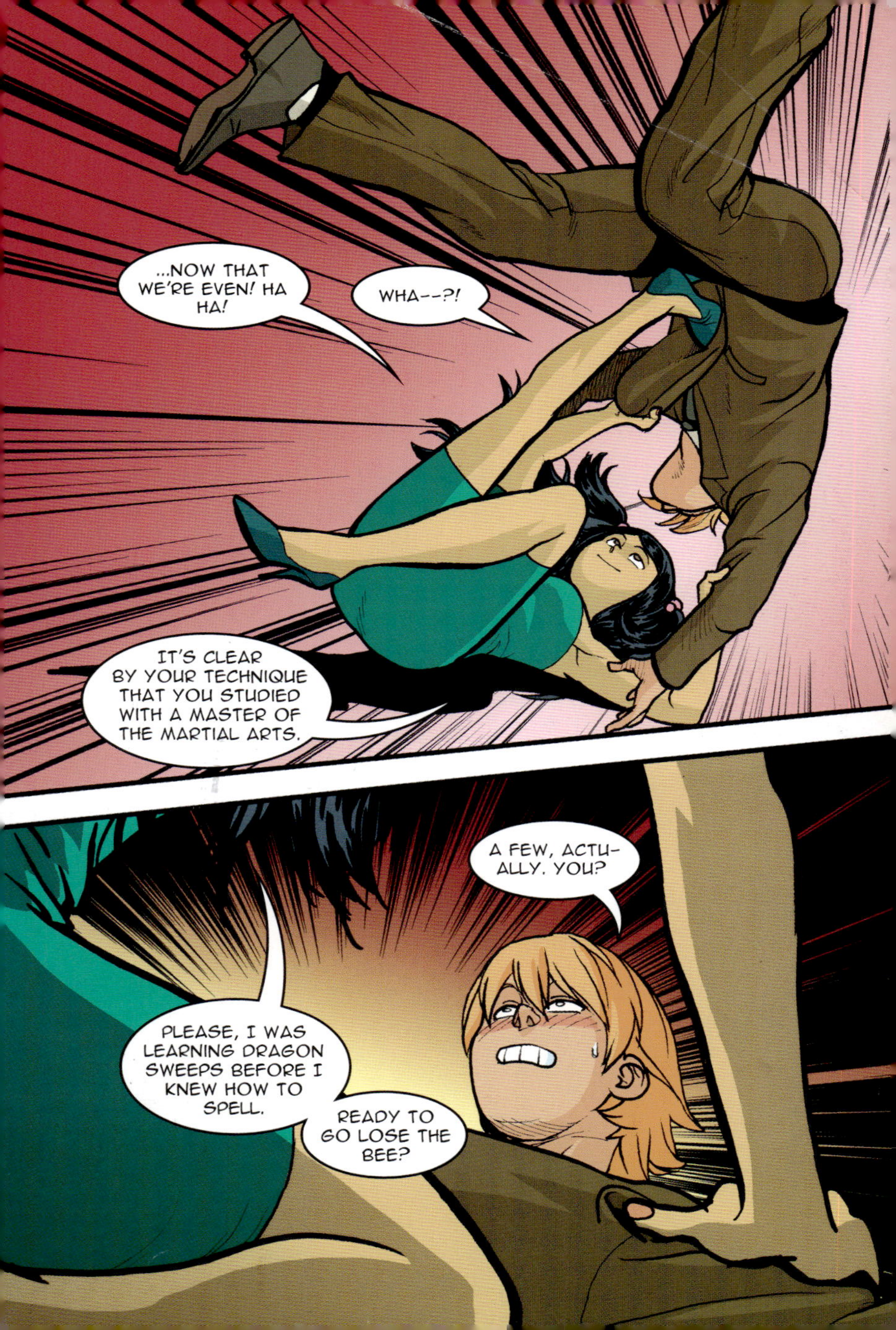
...NOW THAT WE'RE EVEN! HA HA!
WHA--?!
IT'S CLEAR BY YOUR TECHNIQUE THAT YOU STUDIED WITH A MASTER OF THE MARTIAL ARTS.
A FEW, ACTU-ALLY. YOU?
PLEASE, I WAS LEARNING DRAGON SWEEPS BEFORE I KNEW HOW TO SPELL.
READY TO GO LOSE THE BEE?

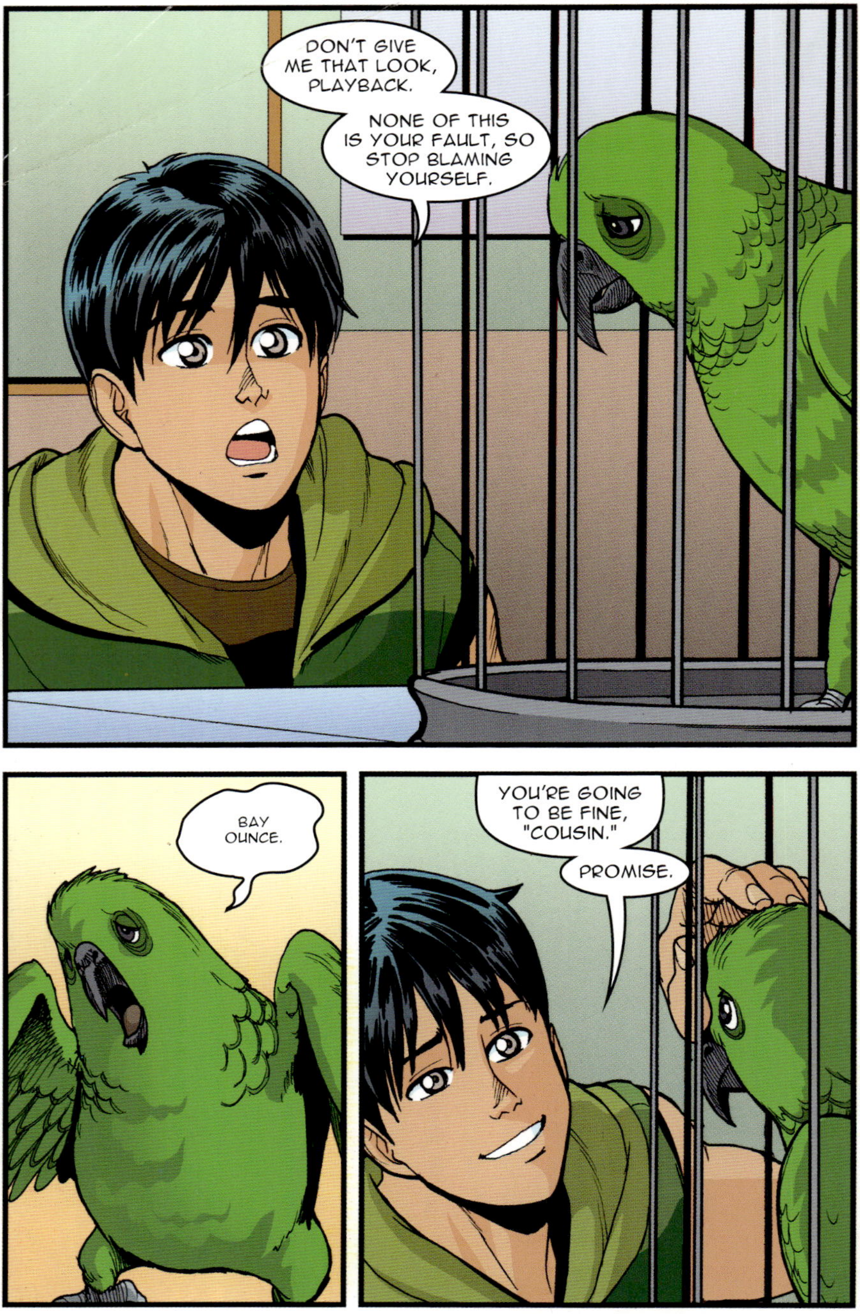
DON'T GIVE ME THAT LOOK, PLAYBACK.
NONE OF THIS IS YOUR FAULT, SO STOP BLAMING YOURSELF.
BAY OUNCE.
YOU'RE GOING TO BE FINE, "COUSIN."
PROMISE.

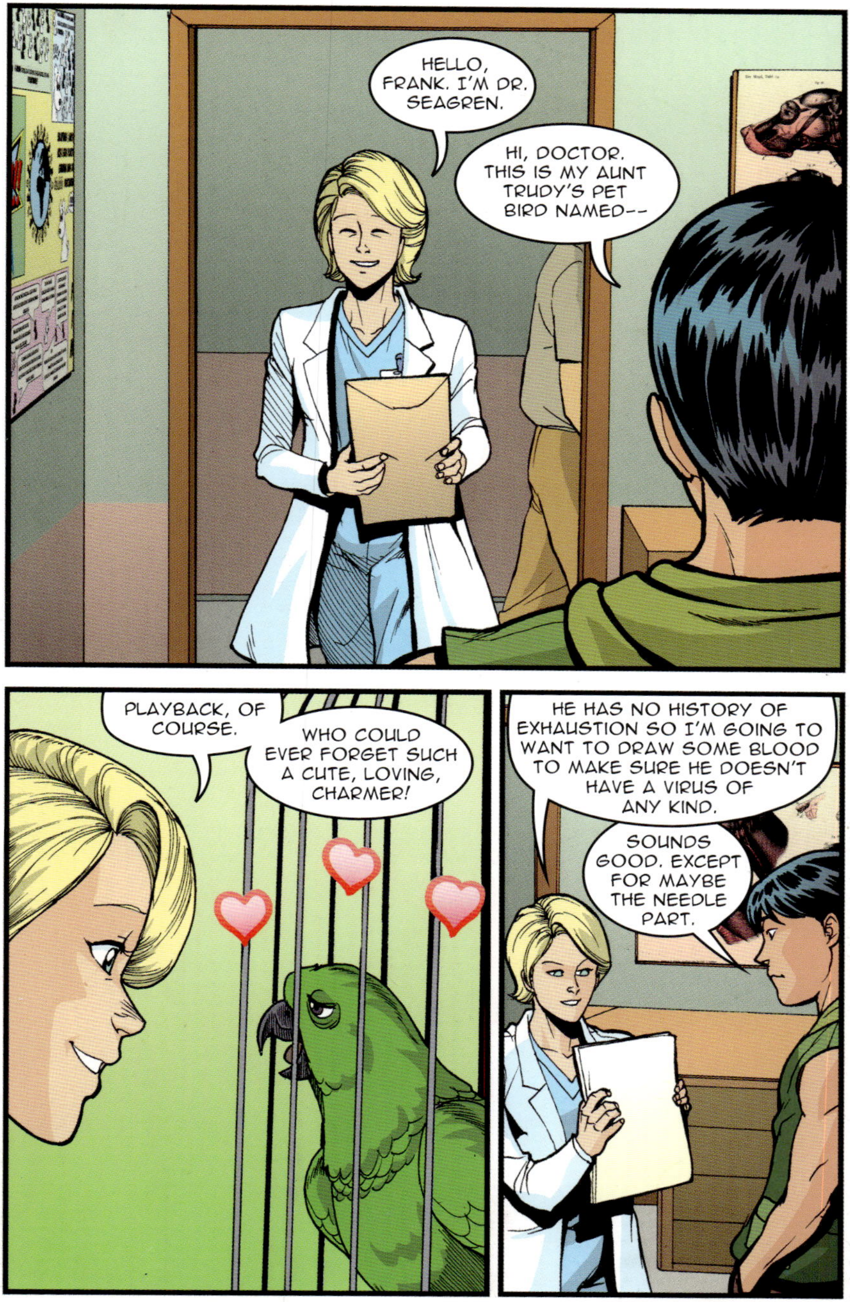
HELLO, FRANK. I'M DR. SEAGREN.
HI, DOCTOR. THIS IS MY AUNT TRUDY'S PET BIRD NAMED--
PLAYBACK, OF COURSE.
WHO COULD EVER FORGET SUCH A CUTE, LOVING, CHARMER!
HE HAS NO HISTORY OF EXHAUSTION SO I'M GOING TO WANT TO DRAW SOME BLOOD TO MAKE SURE HE DOESN'T HAVE A VIRUS OF ANY KIND.
SOUNDS GOOD. EXCEPT FOR MAYBE THE NEEDLE PART.

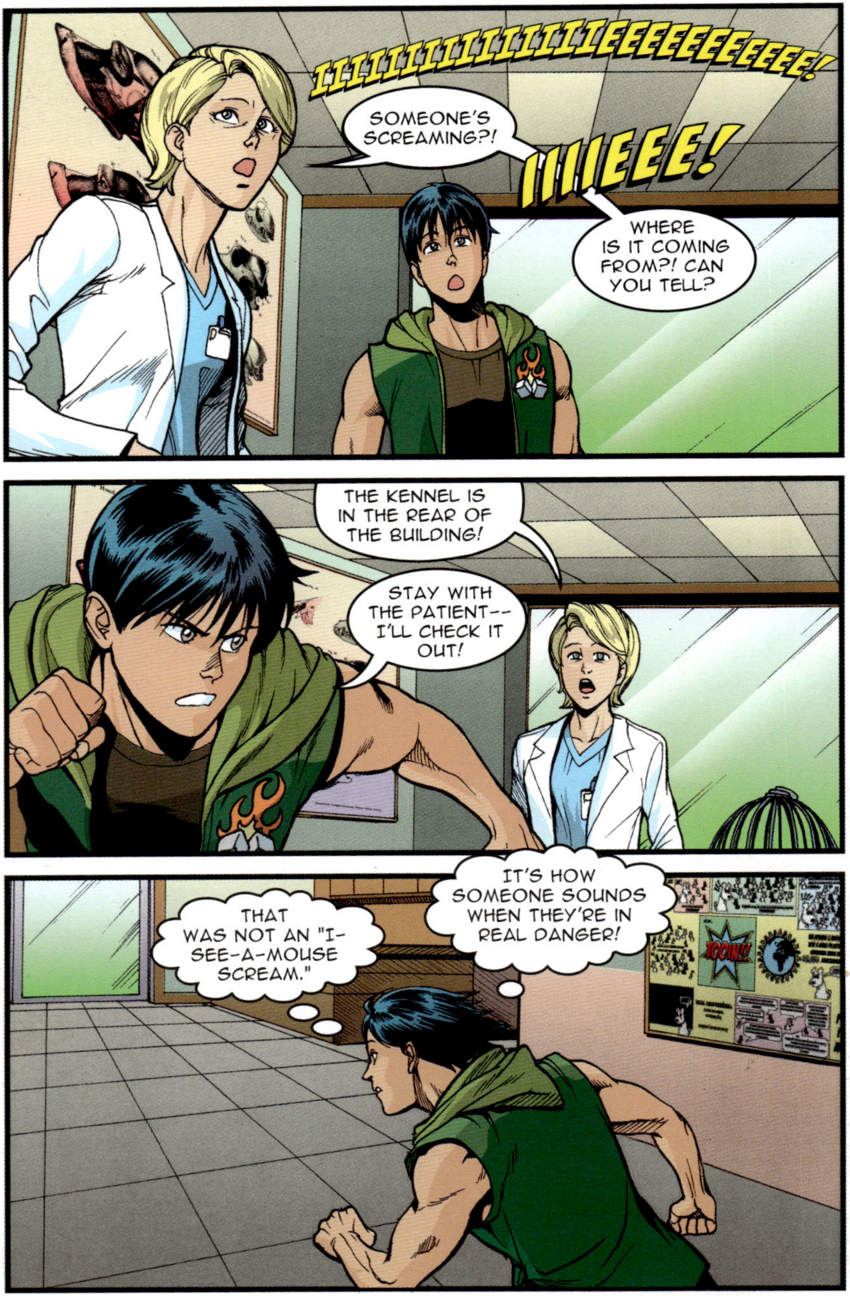
IIIIIIIIIIIIIIIIEEEEEEEEEEE!
SOMEONE'S SCREAMING?!
IIIIEEE!
WHERE IS IT COMING FROM?! CAN YOU TELL?
THE KENNEL IS IN THE REAR OF THE BUILDING!
STAY WITH THE PATIENT-- I'LL CHECK IT OUT!
THAT WAS NOT AN "I-SEE-A-MOUSE SCREAM."
IT'S HOW SOMEONE SOUNDS WHEN THEY'RE IN REAL DANGER!

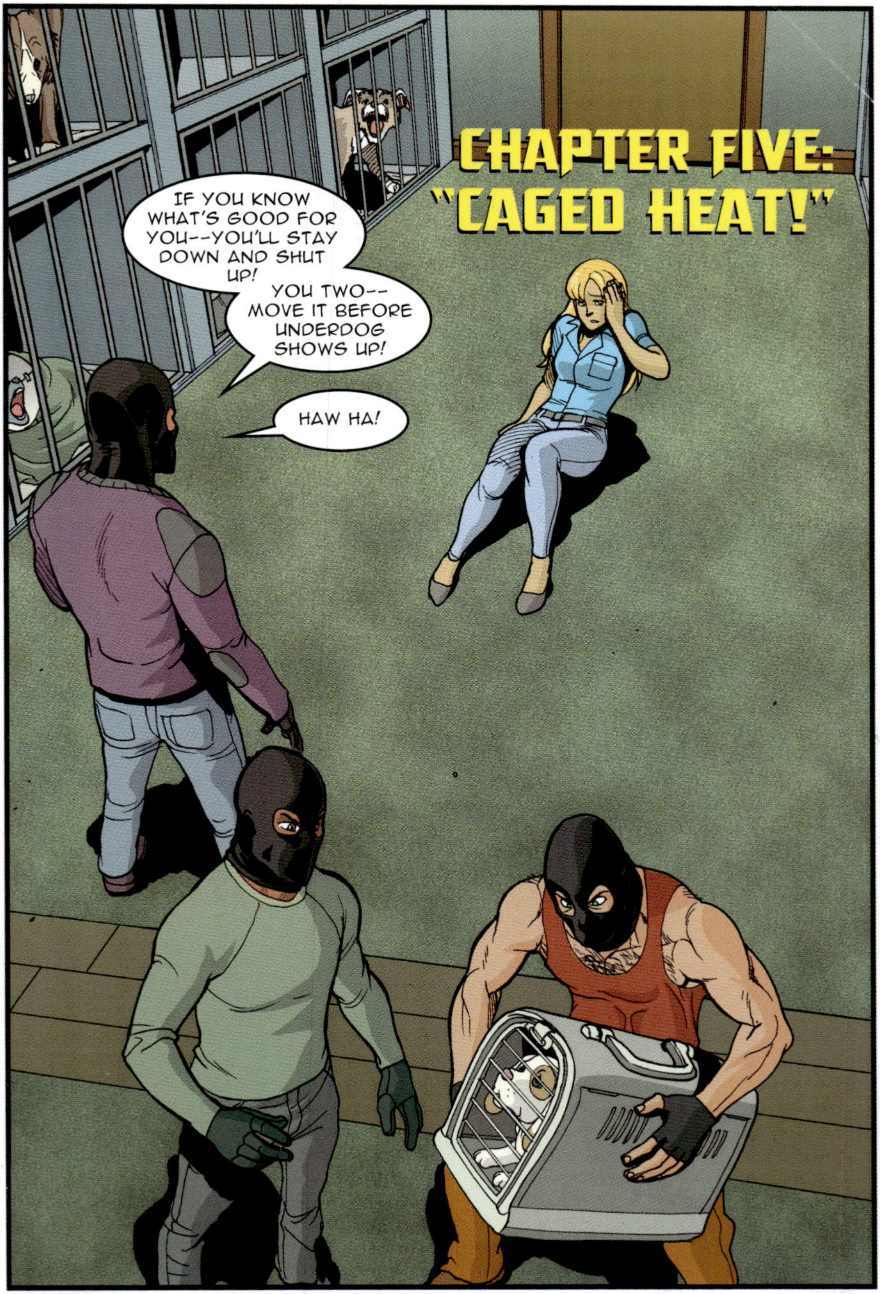
CHAPTER FIVE:
"CAGED HEAT!"
IF YOU KNOW WHAT'S GOOD FOR YOU--YOU'LL STAY DOWN AND SHUT UP!
YOU TWO-- MOVE IT BEFORE UNDERDOG SHOWS UP!
HAW HA!

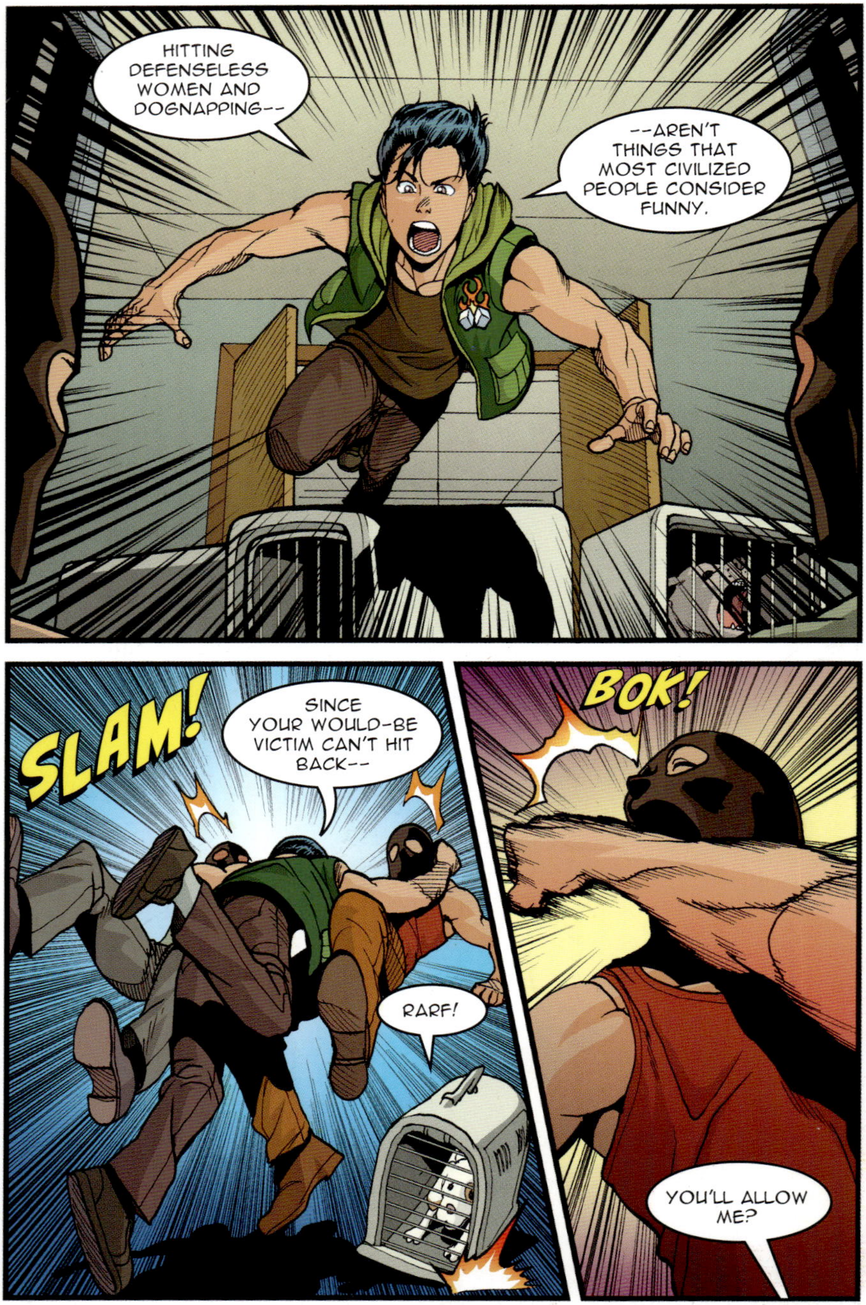
HITTING DEFENSELESS WOMEN AND DOGNAPPING--
--AREN'T THINGS THAT MOST CIVILIZED PEOPLE CONSIDER FUNNY.
SLAM!
SINCE YOUR WOULD-BE VICTIM CAN'T HIT BACK--
RARF!
BOK!
YOU'LL ALLOW ME?

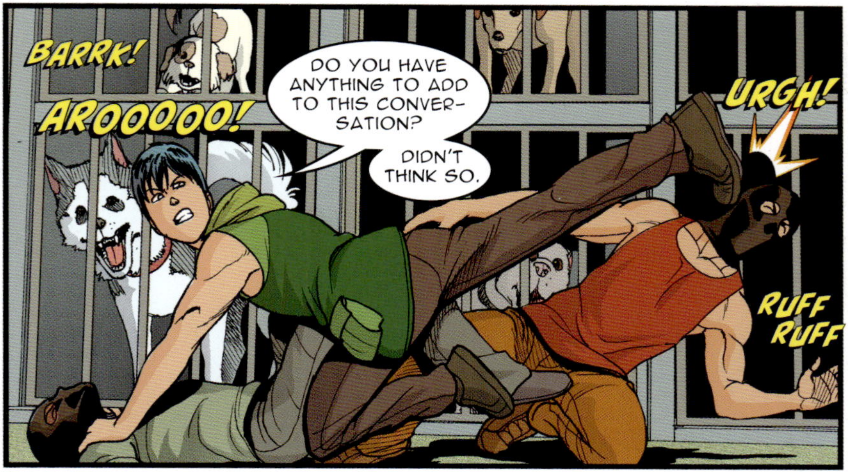
BARRK!
AROOOOO!
DO YOU HAVE ANYTHING TO ADD TO THIS CONVER-SATION?
DIDN'T THINK SO.
URGH!
RUFF RUFF

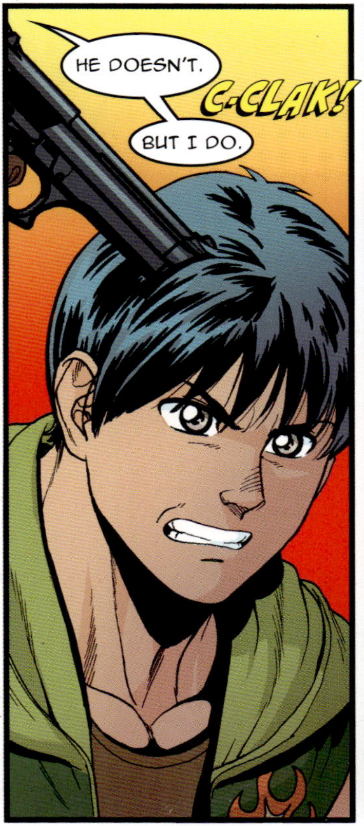
HE DOESN'T.
C-CLAK!
BUT I DO.

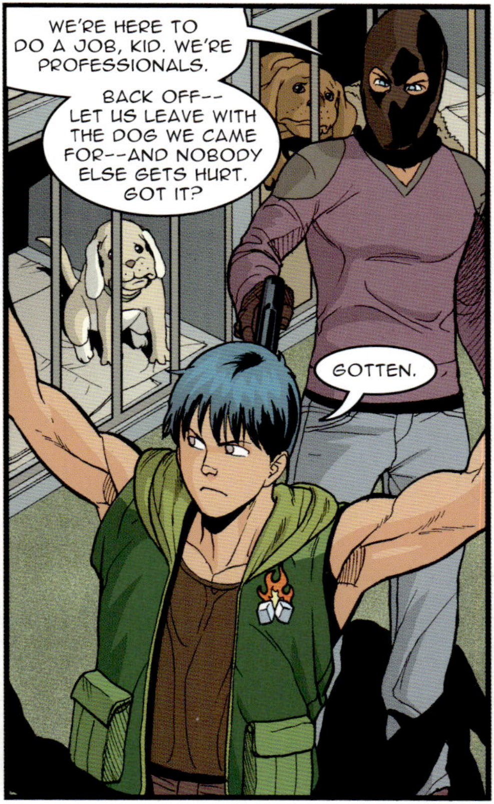
WE'RE HERE TO DO A JOB, KID. WE'RE PROFESSIONALS.
BACK OFF--LET US LEAVE WITH THE DOG WE CAME FOR--AND NOBODY ELSE GETS HURT. GOT IT?
GOTTEN.

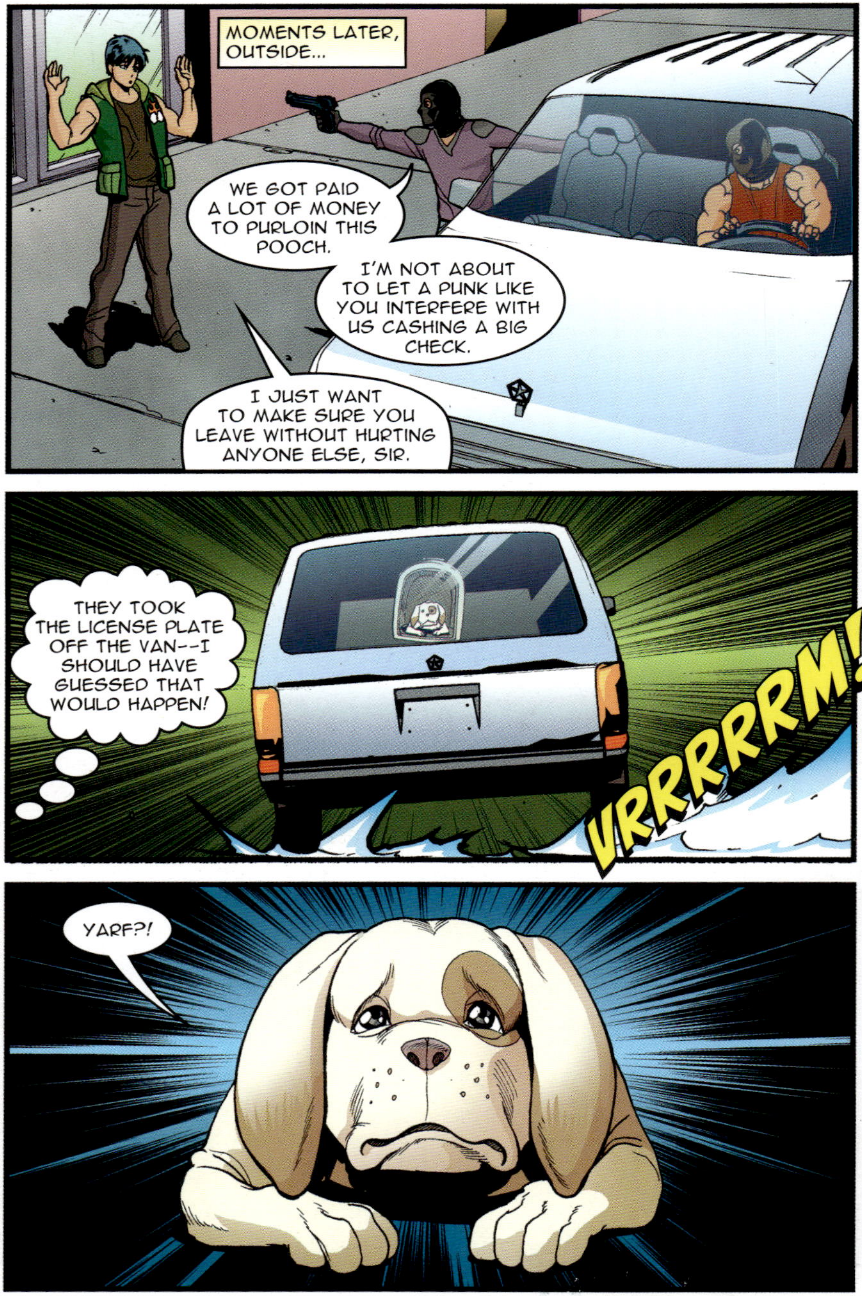

MOMENTS LATER, OUTSIDE...
WE GOT PAID A LOT OF MONEY TO PURLOIN THIS POOCH.
I'M NOT ABOUT TO LET A PUNK LIKE YOU INTERFERE WITH US CASHING A BIG CHECK.
I JUST WANT TO MAKE SURE YOU LEAVE WITHOUT HURTING ANYONE ELSE, SIR.
THEY TOOK THE LICENSE PLATE OFF THE VAN--I SHOULD HAVE GUESSED THAT WOULD HAPPEN!
VRRRRRM!
YARF?!

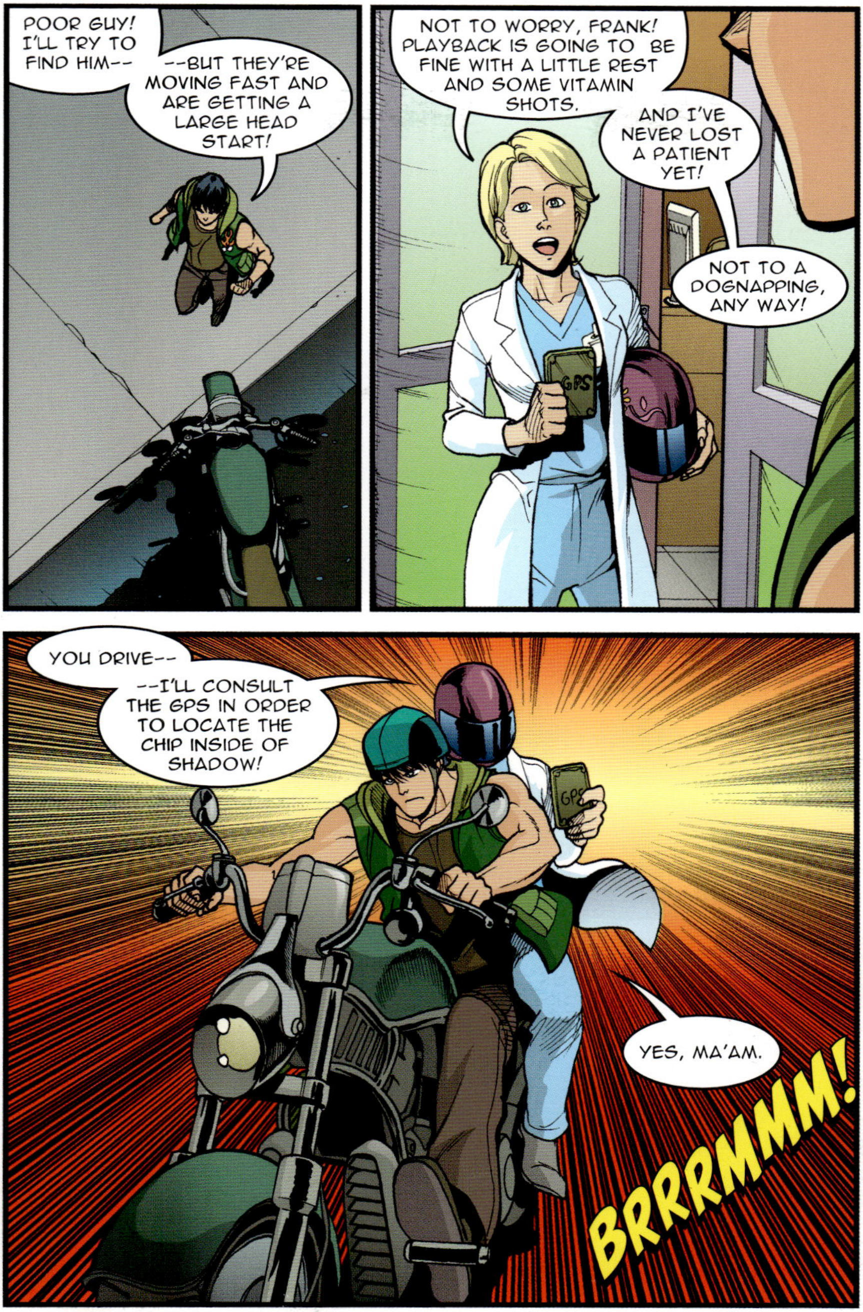
POOR GUY! I'LL TRY TO FIND HIM--
--BUT THEY'RE MOVING FAST AND ARE GETTING A LARGE HEAD START!
NOT TO WORRY, FRANK! PLAYBACK IS GOING TO BE FINE WITH A LITTLE REST AND SOME VITAMIN SHOTS.
AND I'VE NEVER LOST A PATIENT YET!
NOT TO A DOGNAPPING, ANY WAY!
GPS
YOU DRIVE--
--I'LL CONSULT THE GPS IN ORDER TO LOCATE THE CHIP INSIDE OF SHADOW!
GPS
YES, MA'AM.
BRRRMMM!

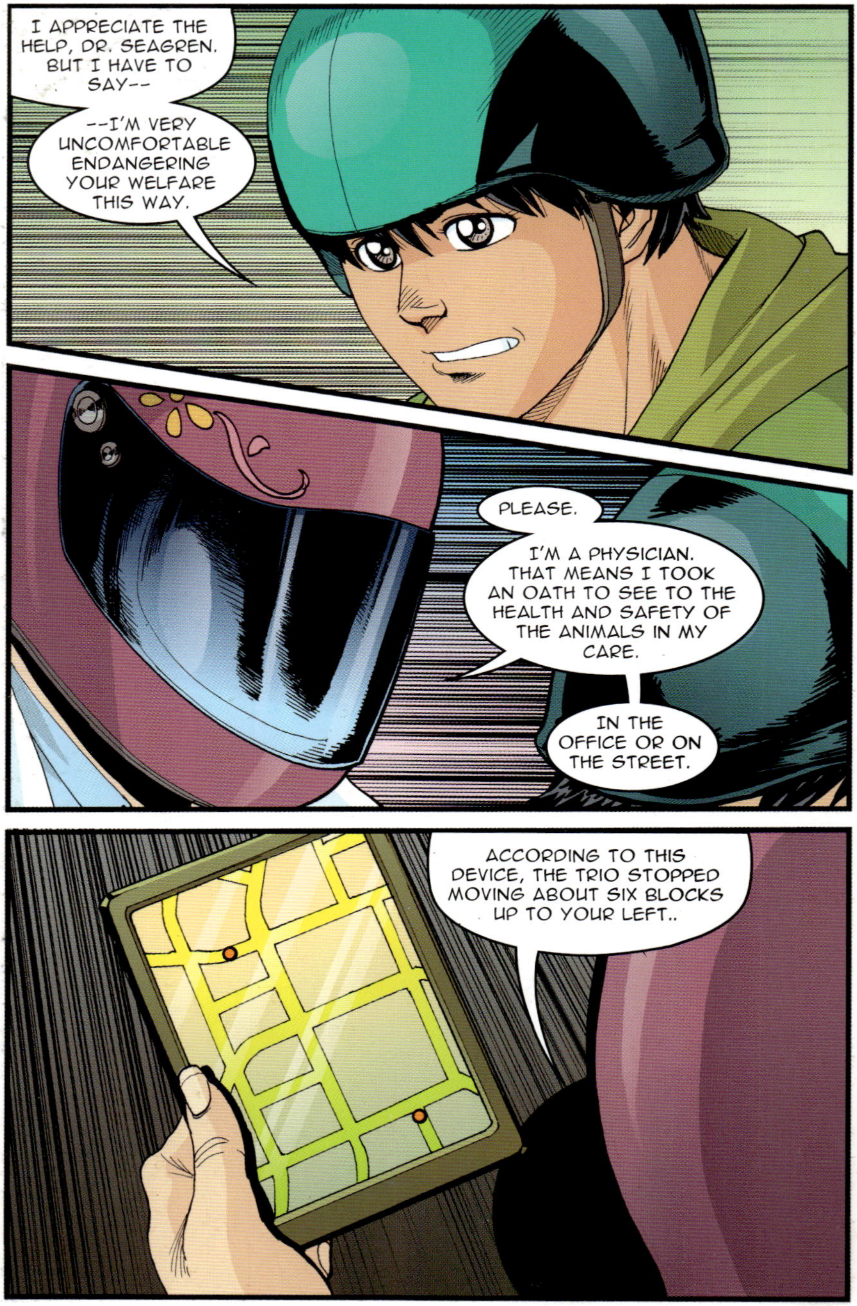

I APPRECIATE THE HELP, DR. SEAGREN. BUT I HAVE TO SAY--
--I'M VERY UNCOMFORTABLE ENDANGERING YOUR WELFARE THIS WAY.
PLEASE.
I'M A PHYSICIAN. THAT MEANS I TOOK AN OATH TO SEE TO THE HEALTH AND SAFETY OF THE ANIMALS IN MY CARE.
IN THE OFFICE OR ON THE STREET.
ACCORDING TO THIS DEVICE, THE TRIO STOPPED MOVING ABOUT SIX BLOCKS UP TO YOUR LEFT..

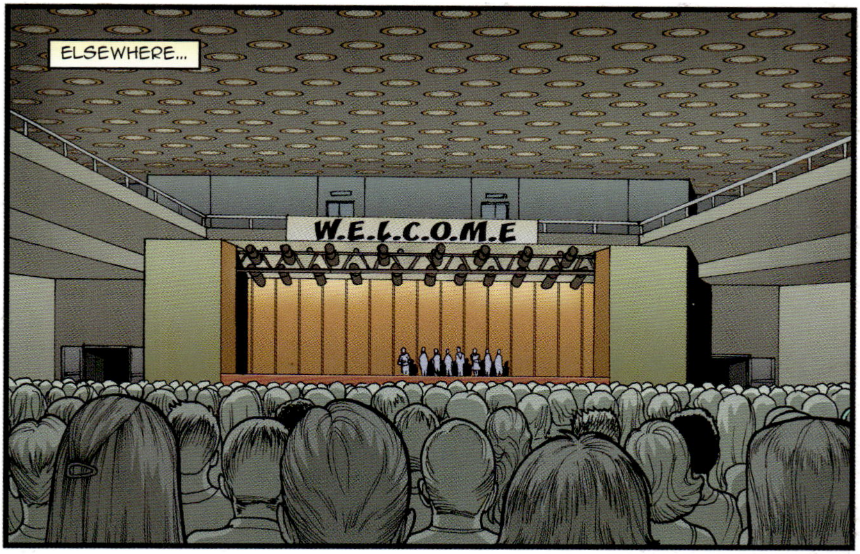
ELSEWHERE...
W.E.L.C.O.M.E

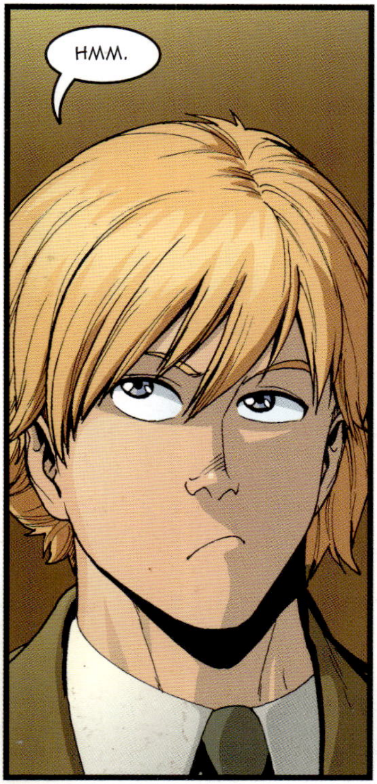
HMM.

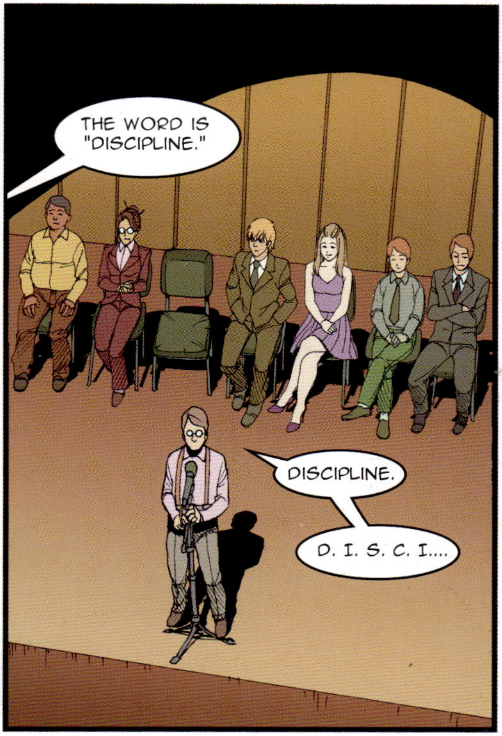
THE WORD IS "DISCIPLINE."
DISCIPLINE.
D. I. S. C. I....

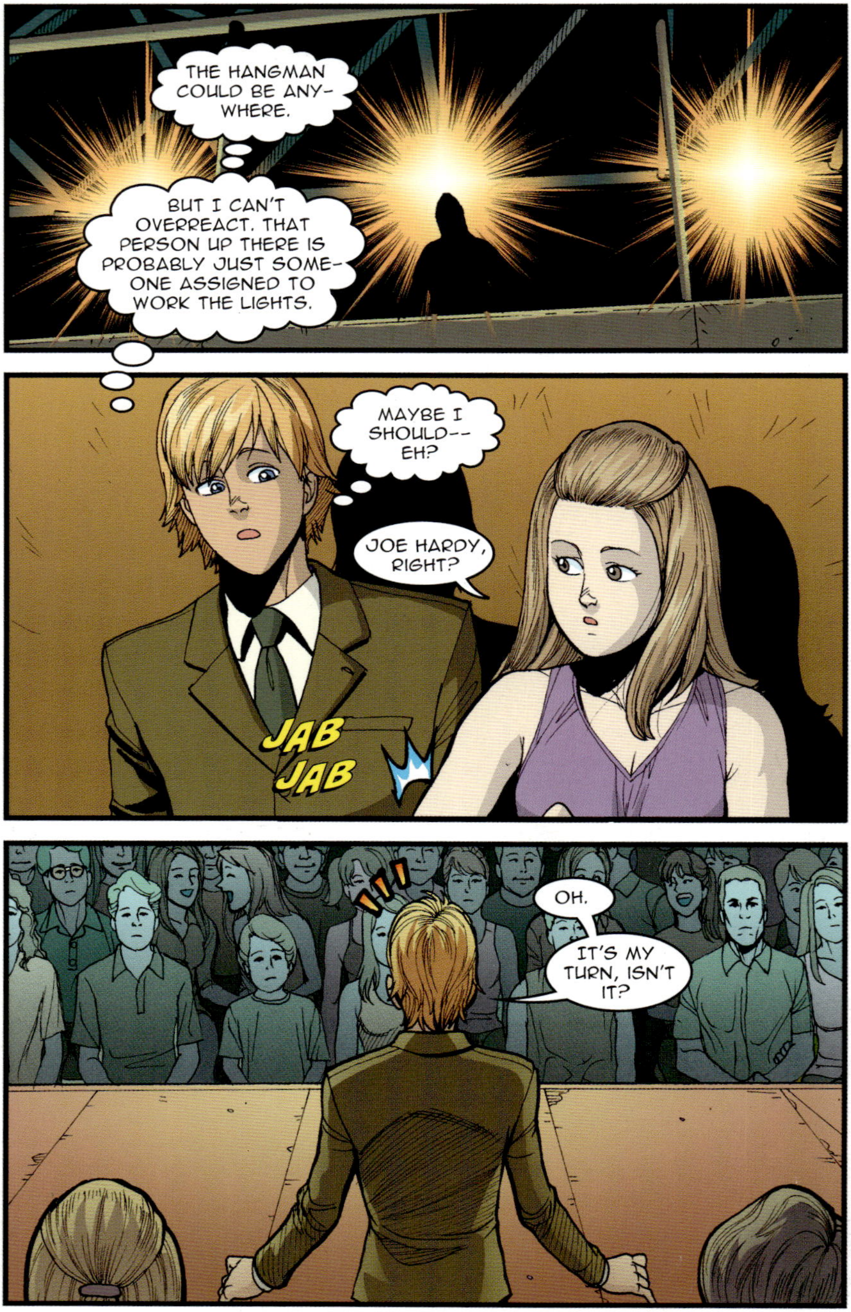
THE HANGMAN COULD BE ANY-WHERE.
BUT I CAN'T OVERREACT. THAT PERSON UP THERE IS PROBABLY JUST SOME-ONE ASSIGNED TO WORK THE LIGHTS.
MAYBE I SHOULD-- EH?
JOE HARDY, RIGHT?
JAB JAB
OH.
IT'S MY TURN, ISN'T IT?

I HAVE SOME DISCRETION AS TO WHETHER TO REPEAT THE WORD OR NOT.

BECAUSE THIS IS THE FIRST ROUND I WILL ALLOW IT THIS ONE AND ONLY TIME.

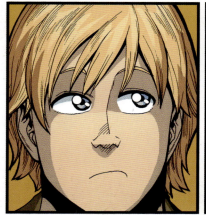

THANK YOU, SIR.

TEE HEE

THE WORD, APPROPRIATELY ENOUGH, IS "CONSCIENTIOUS."

>PHEW<
EASY BREEZY.
C.O.N.S.C.I. E.N.T.I.O.U.S.
THAT IS CORRECT.
CLAP CLAP CLAP
THE NEXT WORD IS "ACQUIT."
I KNOW TAM IS VERY COMPETITIVE...
....BUT WHY IS SHE SUDDENLY SO HORRIFIED?

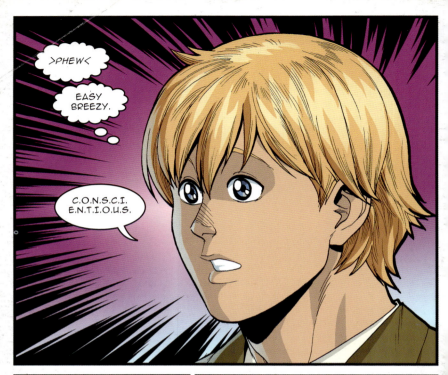

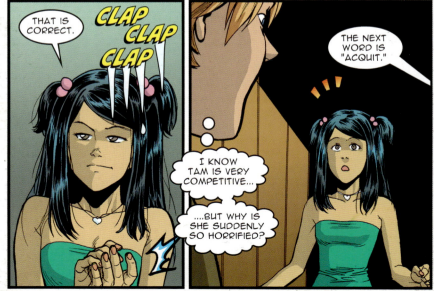

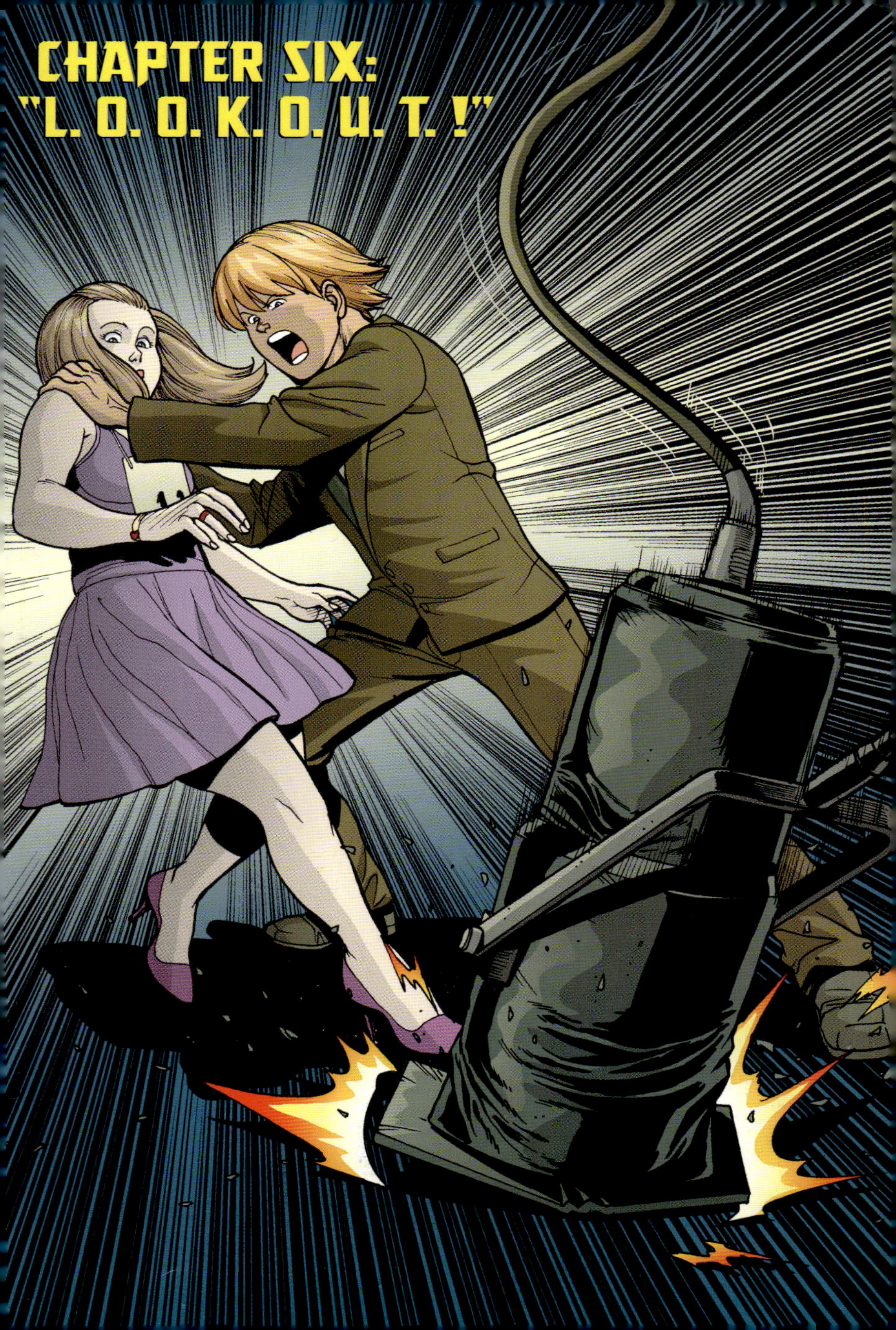
CHAPTER SIX:
"L. O. O. K. O. U. T. !"

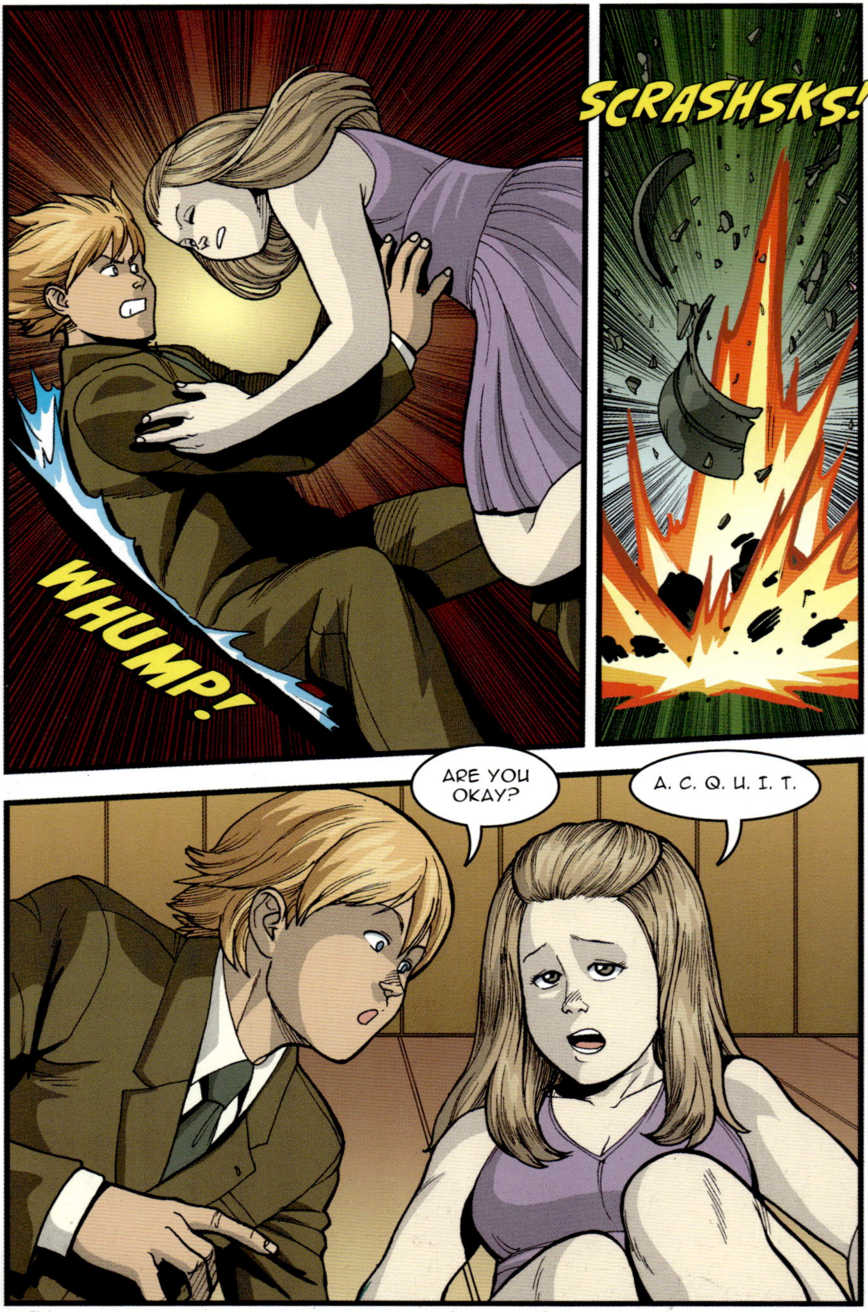
WHUMP!
SCRASHSKS!
ARE YOU OKAY?
A. C. Q. U. I. T.

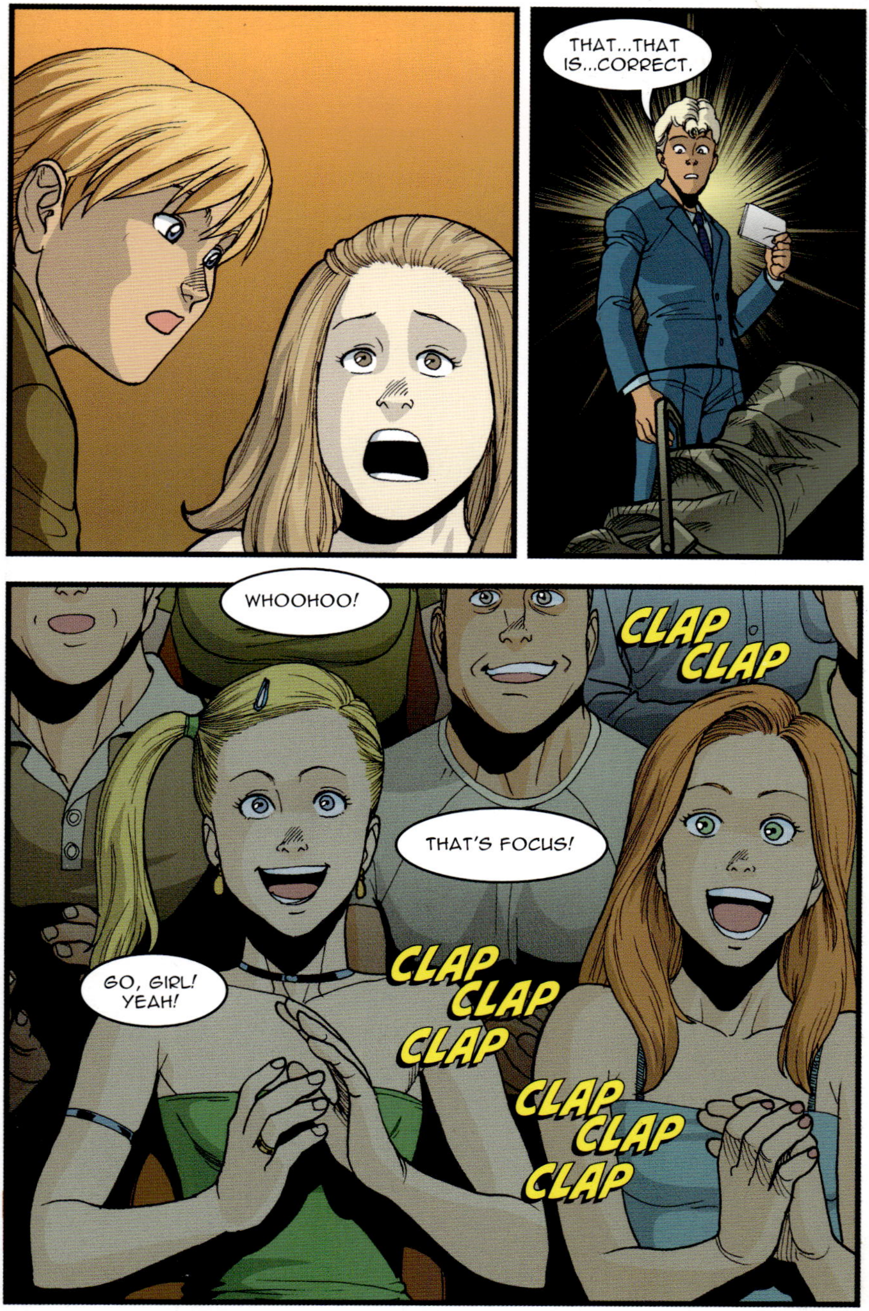
THAT...THAT IS...CORRECT.
WHOOHOO!
CLAP CLAP
THAT'S FOCUS!
GO, GIRL! YEAH!
CLAP CLAP CLAP
CLAP CLAP CLAP

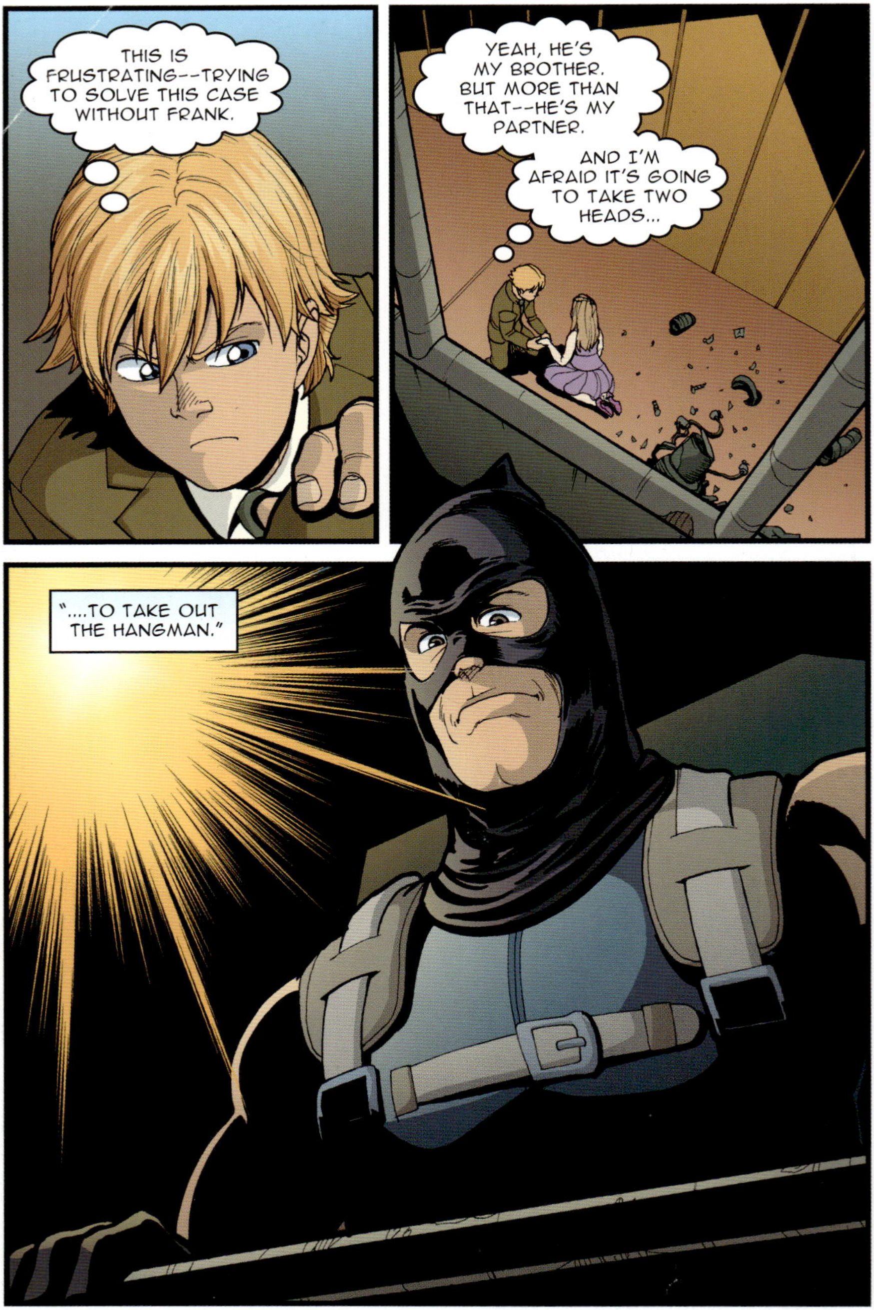
THIS IS FRUSTRATING--TRYING TO SOLVE THIS CASE WITHOUT FRANK.
YEAH, HE'S MY BROTHER. BUT MORE THAN THAT--HE'S MY PARTNER.
AND I'M AFRAID IT'S GOING TO TAKE TWO HEADS...
"....TO TAKE OUT THE HANGMAN."

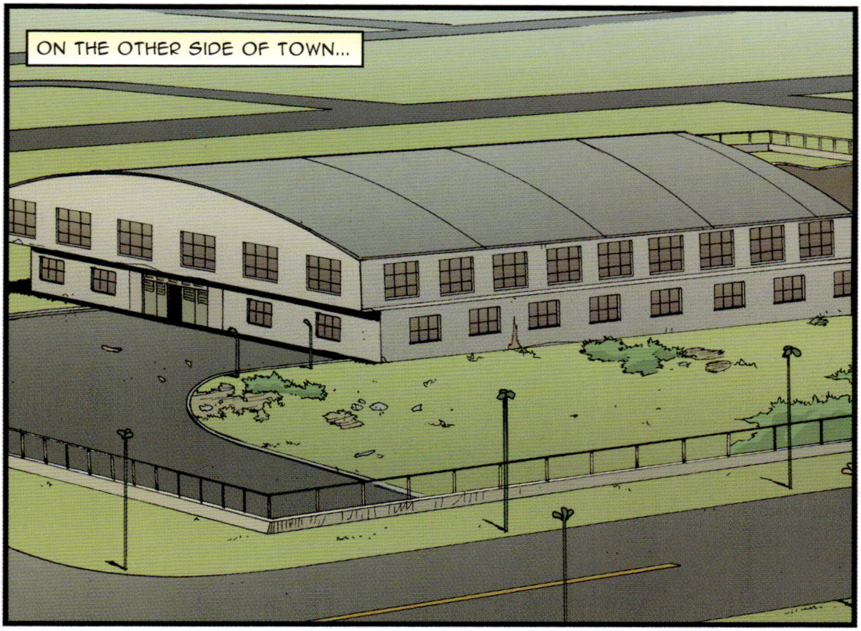
ON THE OTHER SIDE OF TOWN...

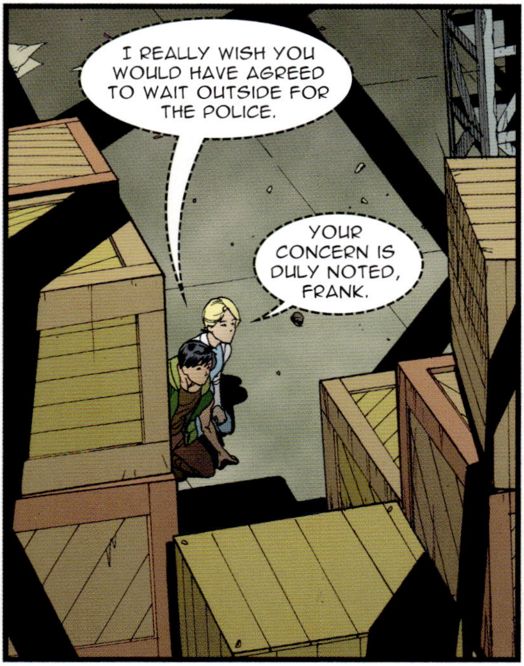
I REALLY WISH YOU WOULD HAVE AGREED TO WAIT OUTSIDE FOR THE POLICE.
YOUR CONCERN IS DULY NOTED, FRANK.

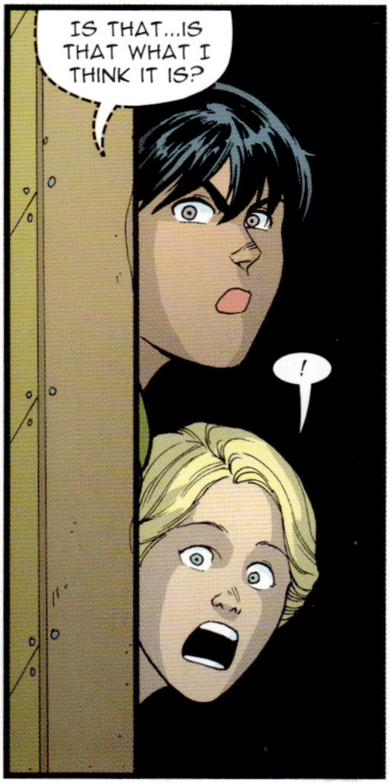
IS THAT...IS THAT WHAT I THINK IT IS?
!

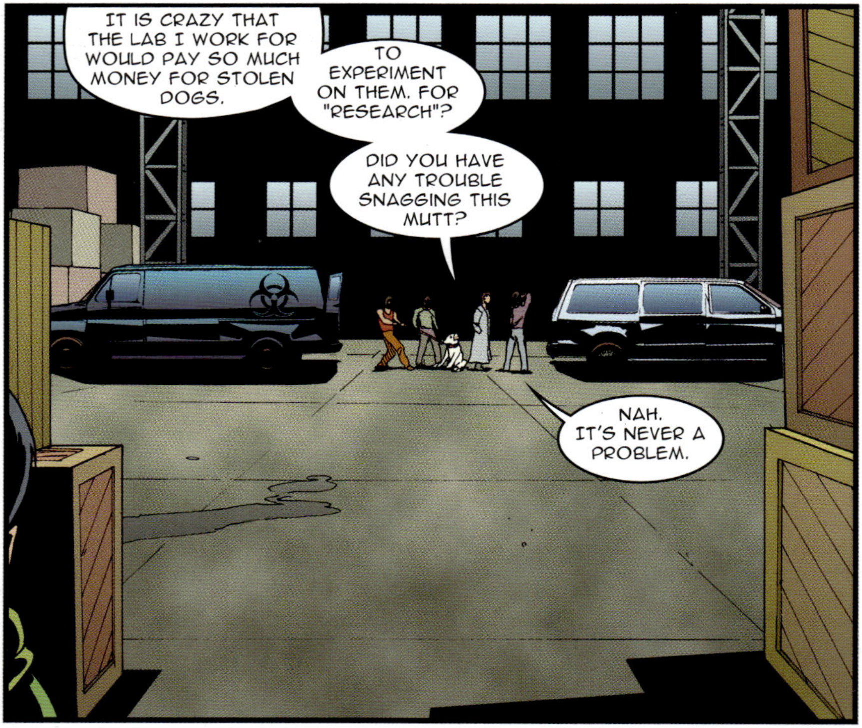
IT IS CRAZY THAT THE LAB I WORK FOR WOULD PAY SO MUCH MONEY FOR STOLEN DOGS.
TO EXPERIMENT ON THEM. FOR "RESEARCH"?
DID YOU HAVE ANY TROUBLE SNAGGING THIS MUTT?
NAH. IT'S NEVER A PROBLEM.

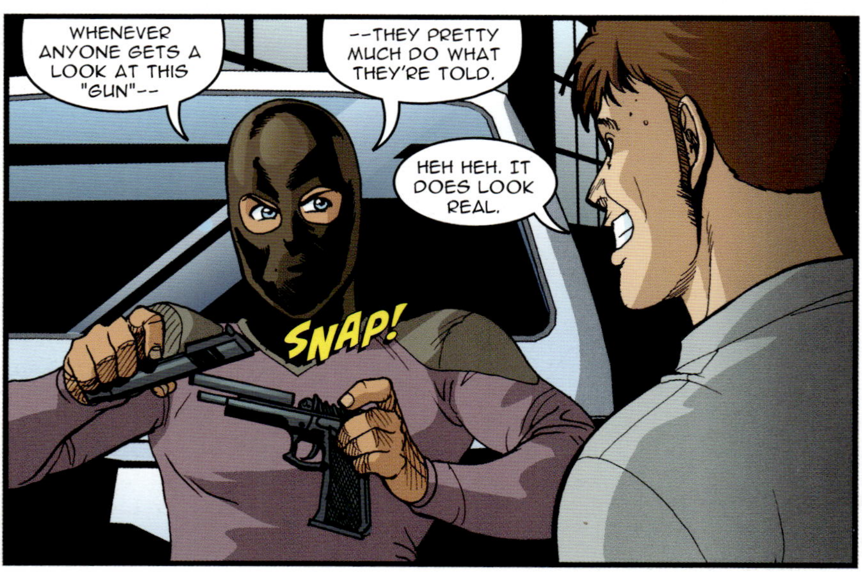
WHENEVER ANYONE GETS A LOOK AT THIS "GUN"--
--THEY PRETTY MUCH DO WHAT THEY'RE TOLD.
HEH HEH. IT DOES LOOK REAL.
SNAP!

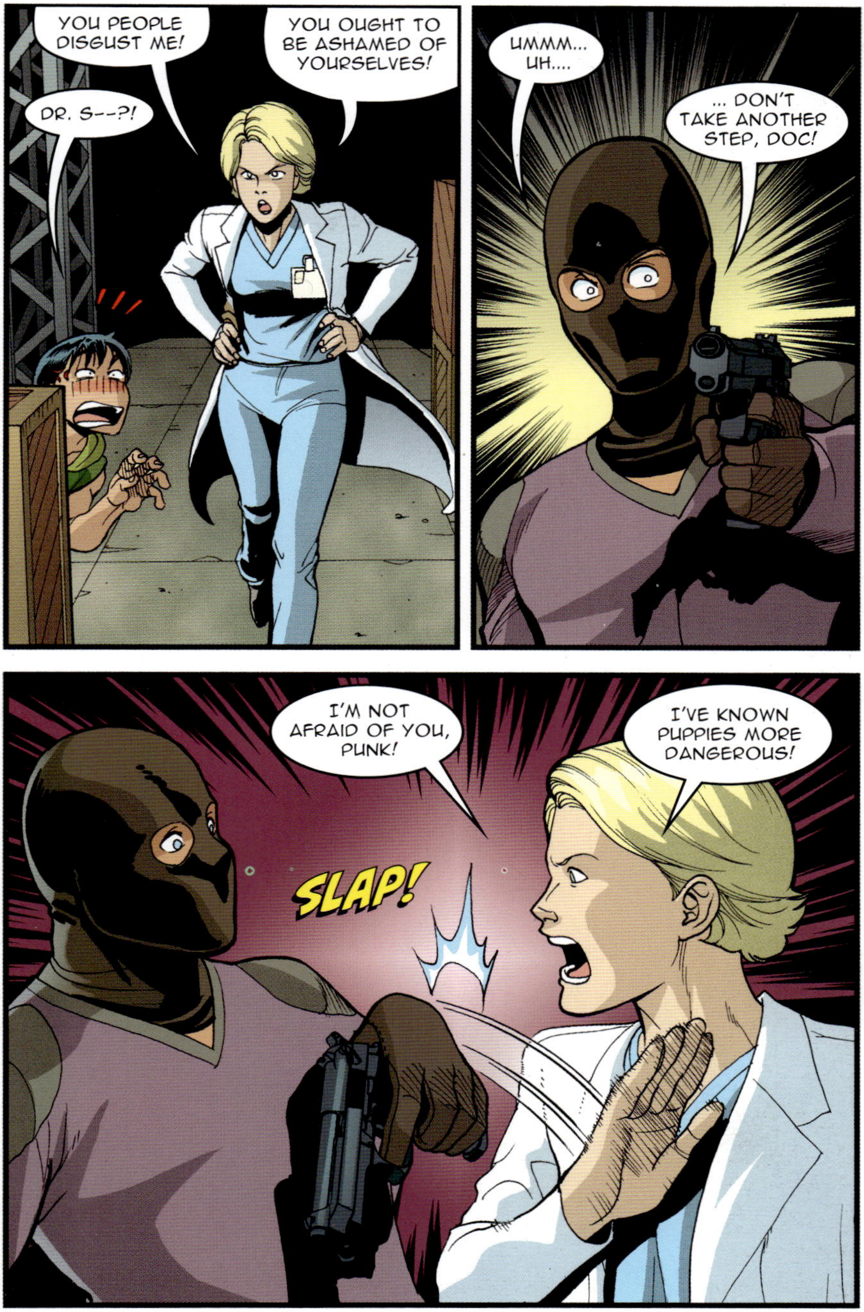
YOU PEOPLE DISGUST ME!
DR. S--?!
YOU OUGHT TO BE ASHAMED OF YOURSELVES!
UMMM... UH....
... DON'T TAKE ANOTHER STEP, DOC!
I'M NOT AFRAID OF YOU, PUNK!
SLAP!
I'VE KNOWN PUPPIES MORE DANGEROUS!

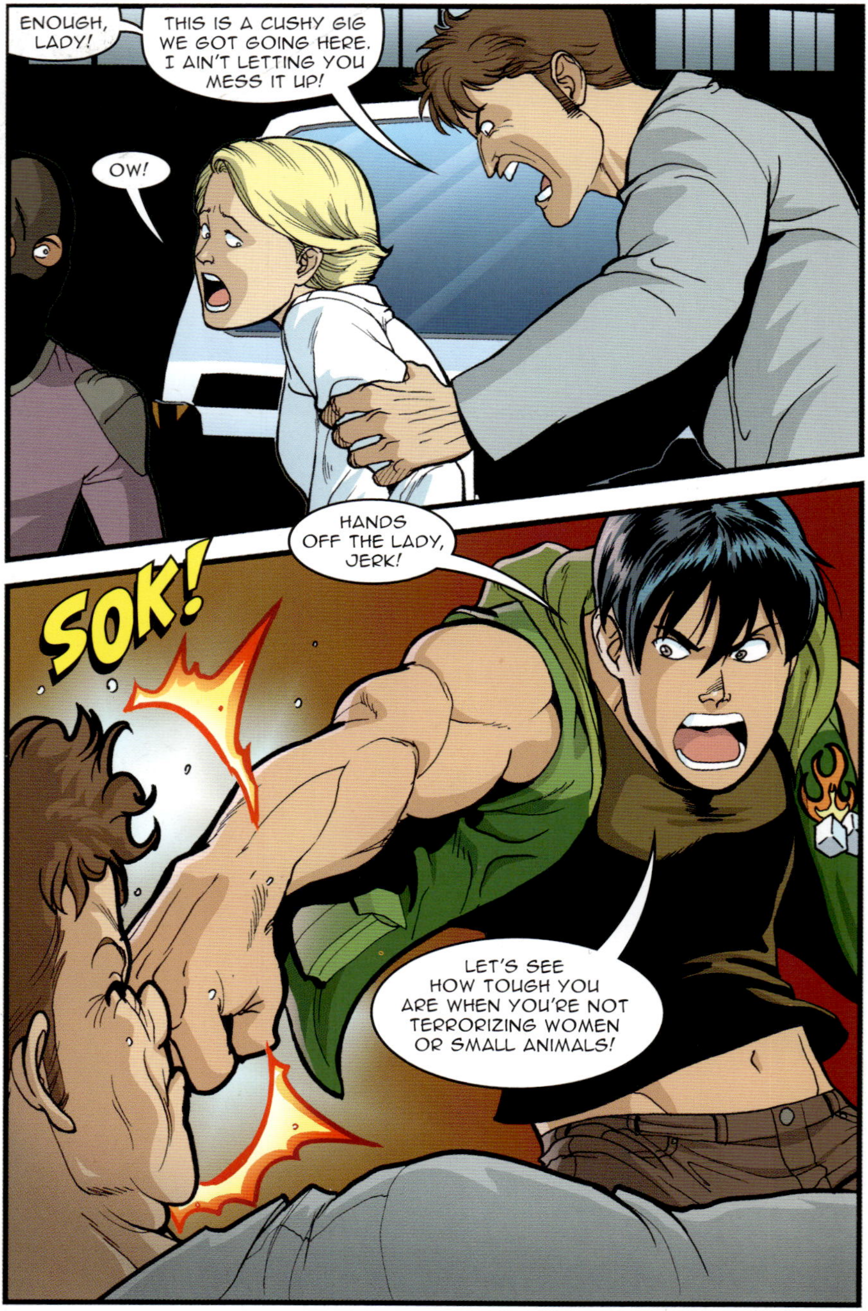
ENOUGH, LADY!
THIS IS A CUSHY GIG WE GOT GOING HERE. I AIN'T LETTING YOU MESS IT UP!
OW!
HANDS OFF THE LADY, JERK!
SOK!
LET'S SEE HOW TOUGH YOU ARE WHEN YOU'RE NOT TERRORIZING WOMEN OR SMALL ANIMALS!

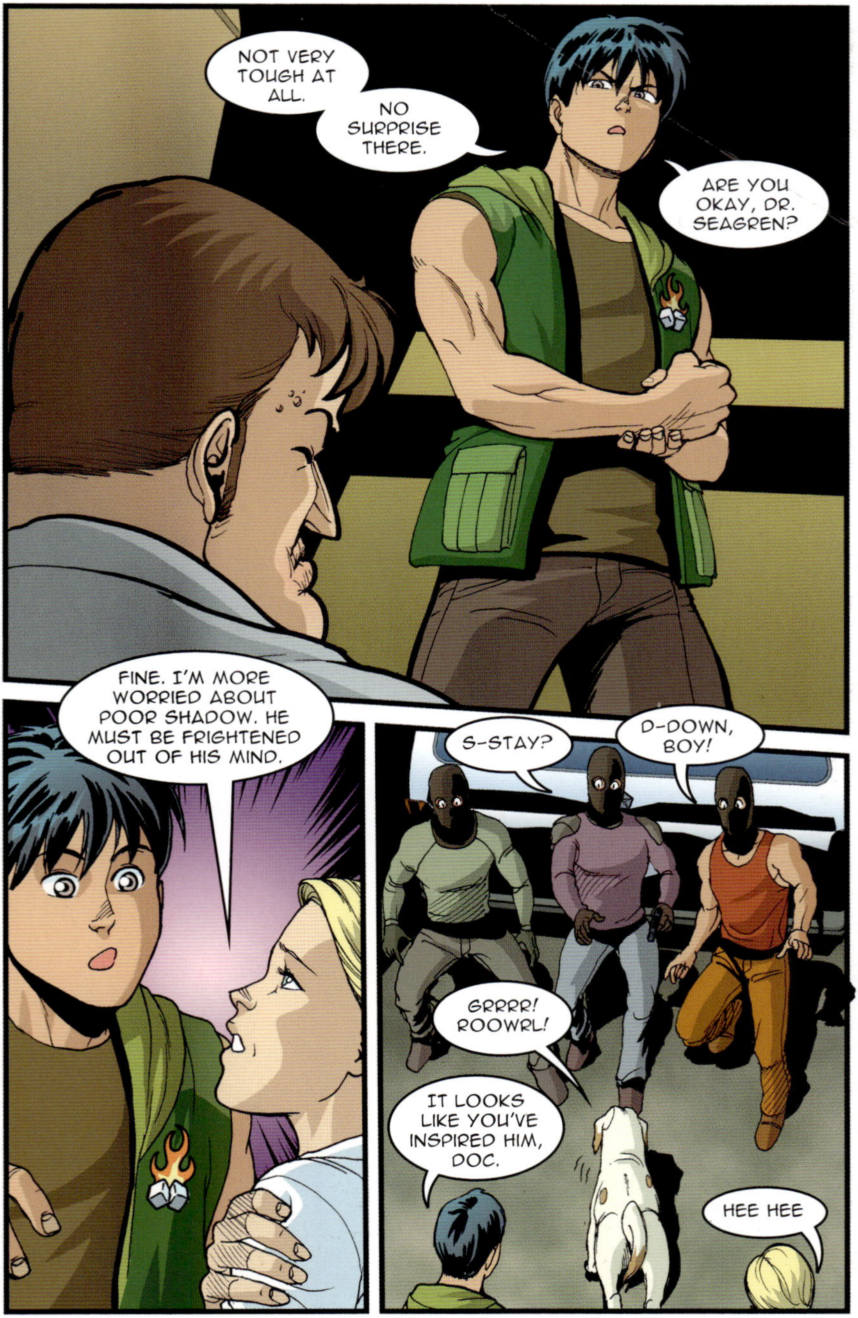
NOT VERY TOUGH AT ALL.
NO SURPRISE THERE.
ARE YOU OKAY, DR. SEAGREN?
FINE. I'M MORE WORRIED ABOUT POOR SHADOW. HE MUST BE FRIGHTENED OUT OF HIS MIND.
S-STAY?
D-DOWN, BOY!
GRRRR! ROOWRL!
IT LOOKS LIKE YOU'VE INSPIRED HIM, DOC.
HEE HEE

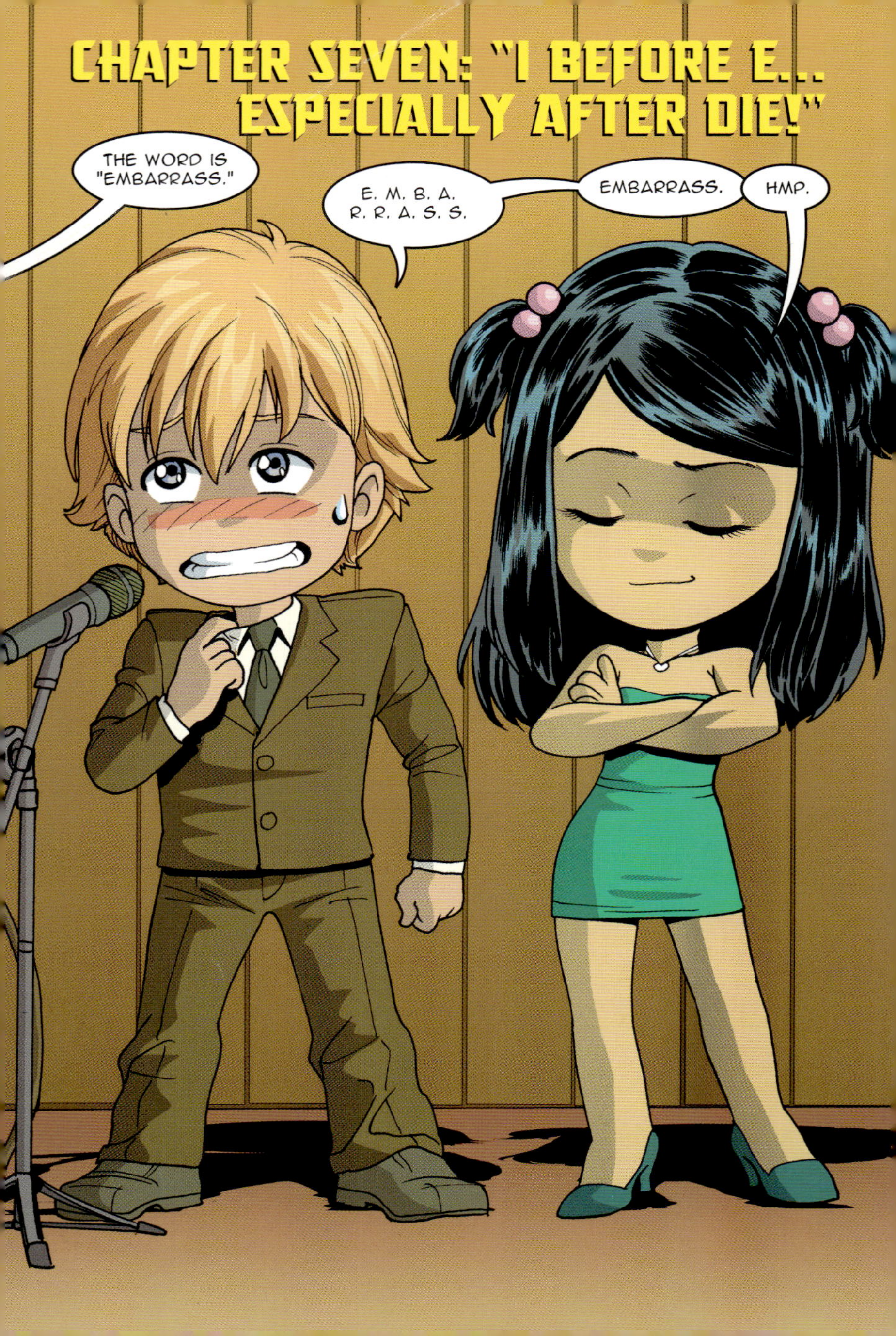
CHAPTER SEVEN: "I BEFORE E... ESPECIALLY AFTER DIE!"
THE WORD IS "EMBARRASS."
E. M. B. A. R. R. A. S. S.
EMBARRASS.
HMP.

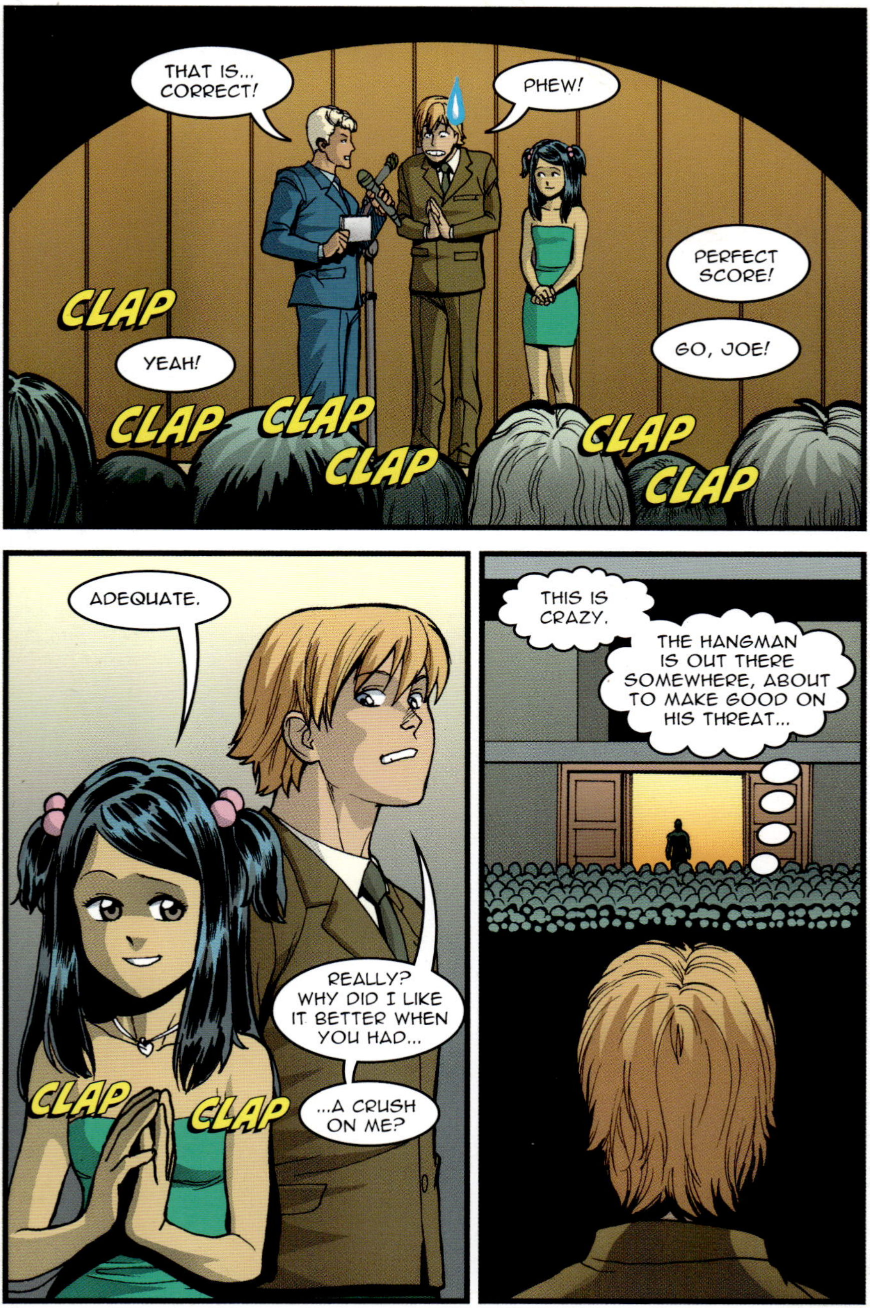
THAT IS... CORRECT!
PHEW!
PERFECT SCORE!
GO, JOE!
YEAH!
CLAP
CLAP
CLAP
CLAP
CLAP
CLAP
ADEQUATE.
REALLY? WHY DID I LIKE IT BETTER WHEN YOU HAD...
...A CRUSH ON ME?
CLAP
CLAP
THIS IS CRAZY.
THE HANGMAN IS OUT THERE SOMEWHERE, ABOUT TO MAKE GOOD ON HIS THREAT...

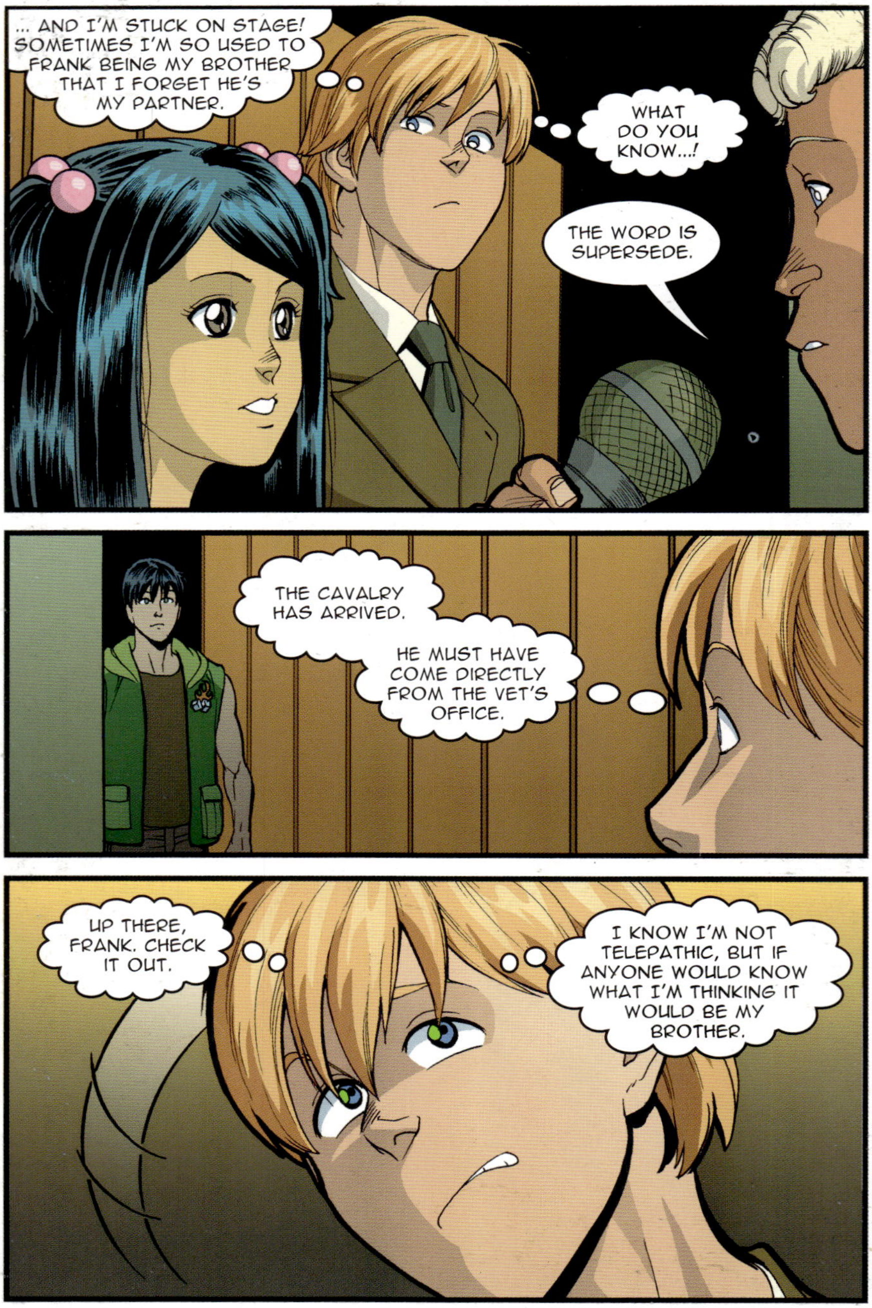
... AND I'M STUCK ON STAGE! SOMETIMES I'M SO USED TO FRANK BEING MY BROTHER THAT I FORGET HE'S MY PARTNER.
WHAT DO YOU KNOW...!
THE WORD IS SUPERSEDE.
THE CAVALRY HAS ARRIVED.
HE MUST HAVE COME DIRECTLY FROM THE VET'S OFFICE.
UP THERE, FRANK. CHECK IT OUT.
I KNOW I'M NOT TELEPATHIC, BUT IF ANYONE WOULD KNOW WHAT I'M THINKING IT WOULD BE MY BROTHER.

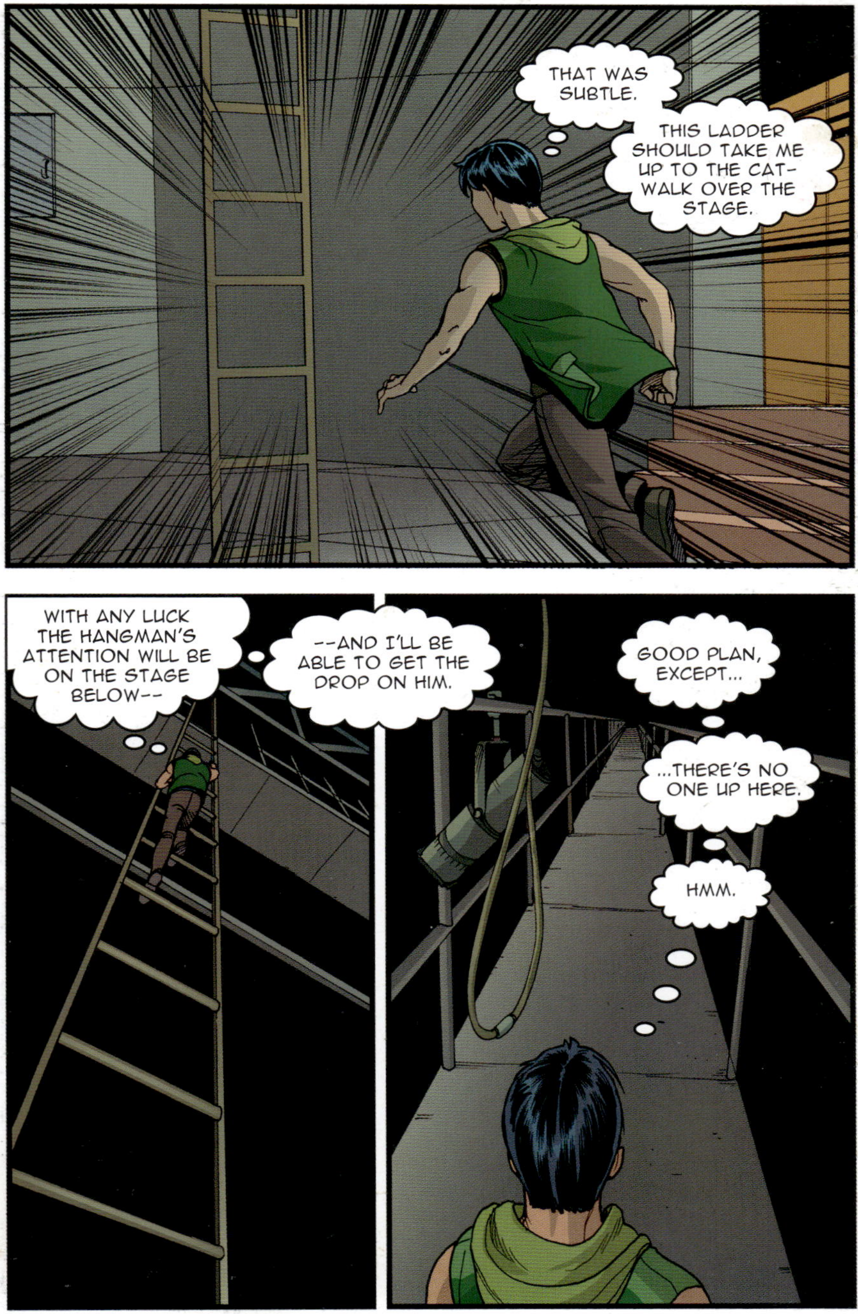
THAT WAS SUBTLE.
THIS LADDER SHOULD TAKE ME UP TO THE CAT-WALK OVER THE STAGE.
WITH ANY LUCK THE HANGMAN'S ATTENTION WILL BE ON THE STAGE BELOW--
--AND I'LL BE ABLE TO GET THE DROP ON HIM.
GOOD PLAN, EXCEPT...
...THERE'S NO ONE UP HERE.
HMM.

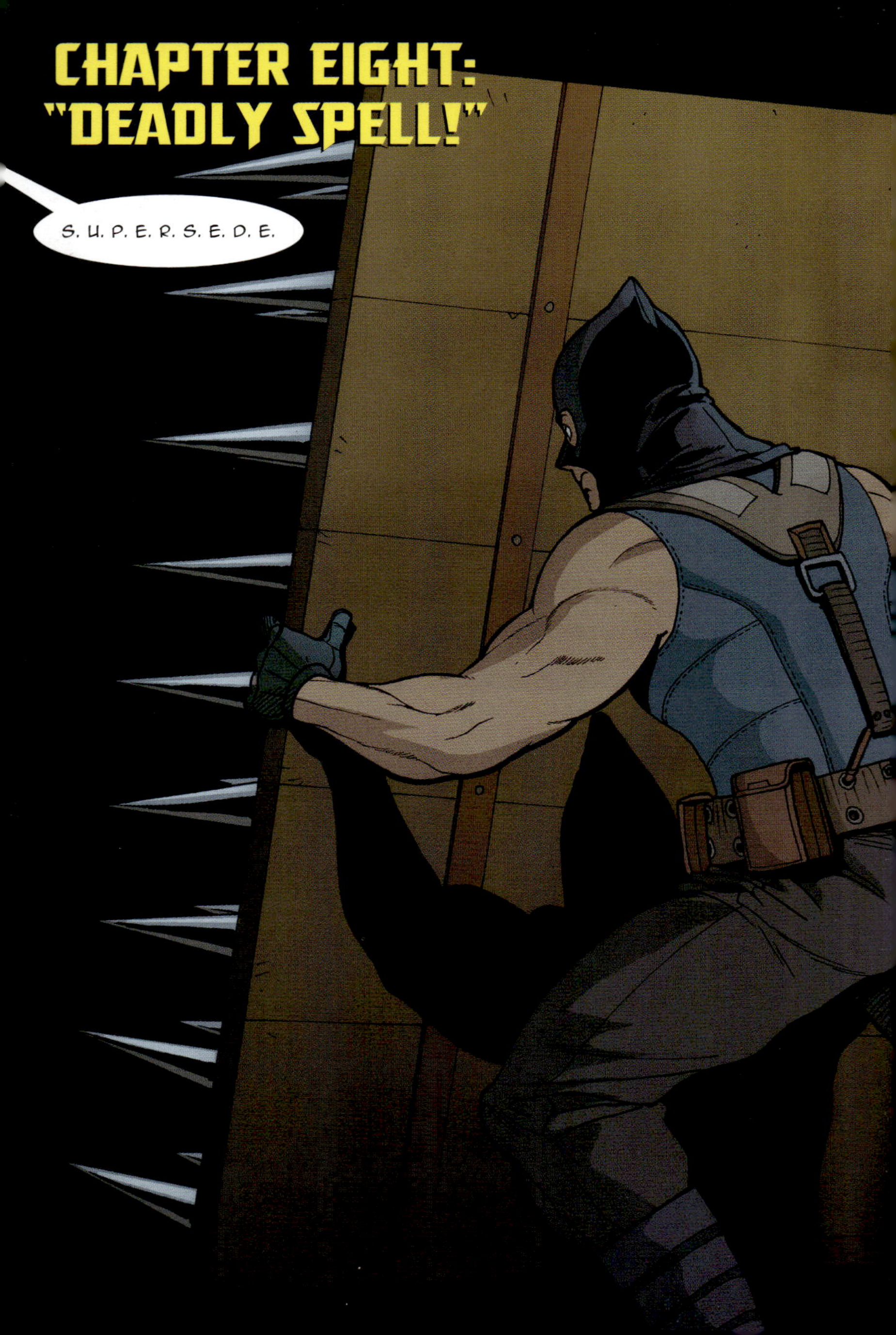
CHAPTER EIGHT: "DEADLY SPELL!"
S. U. P. E. R. S. E. D. E.

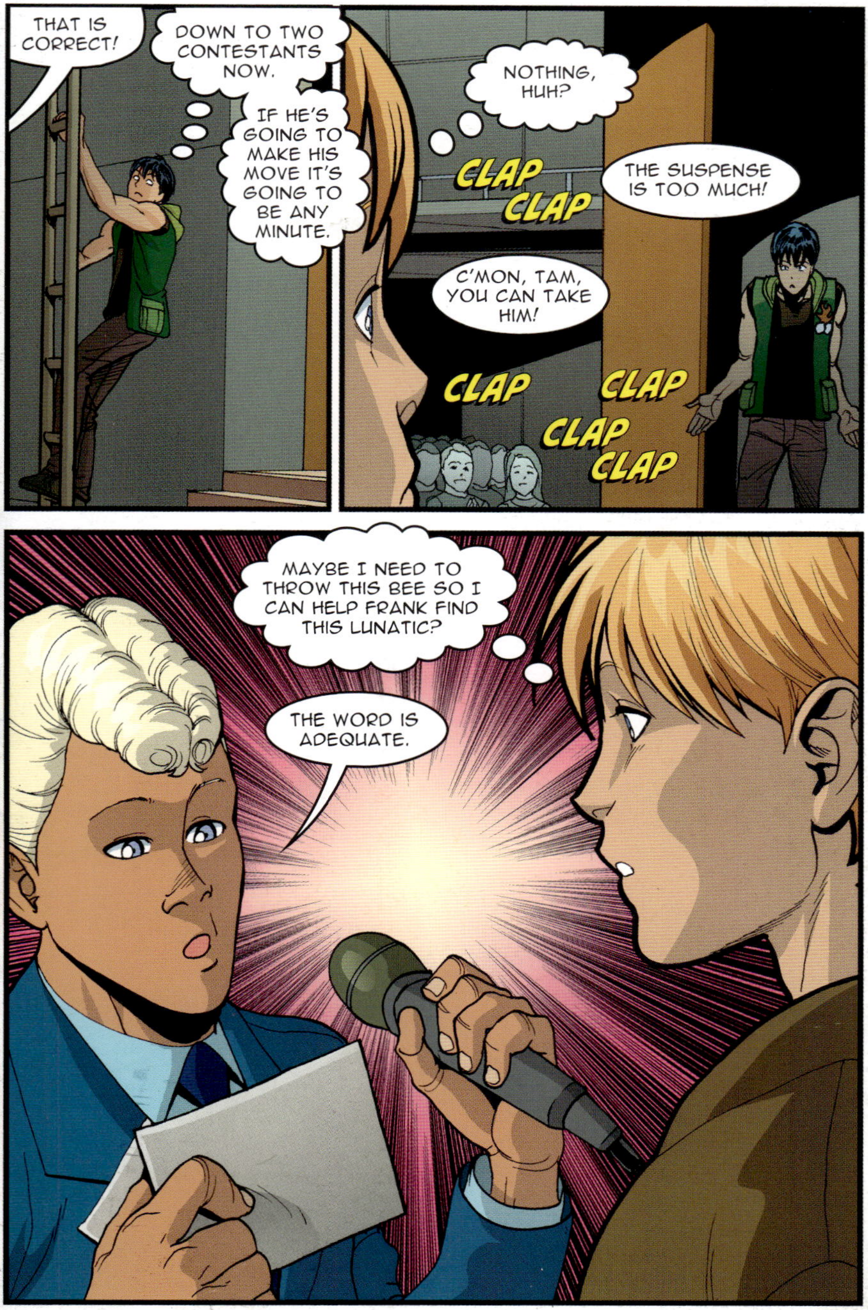
THAT IS CORRECT!
DOWN TO TWO CONTESTANTS NOW.
IF HE'S GOING TO MAKE HIS MOVE IT'S GOING TO BE ANY MINUTE.
NOTHING, HUH?
CLAP CLAP
THE SUSPENSE IS TOO MUCH!
C'MON, TAM, YOU CAN TAKE HIM!
CLAP CLAP CLAP CLAP
MAYBE I NEED TO THROW THIS BEE SO I CAN HELP FRANK FIND THIS LUNATIC?
THE WORD IS ADEQUATE.

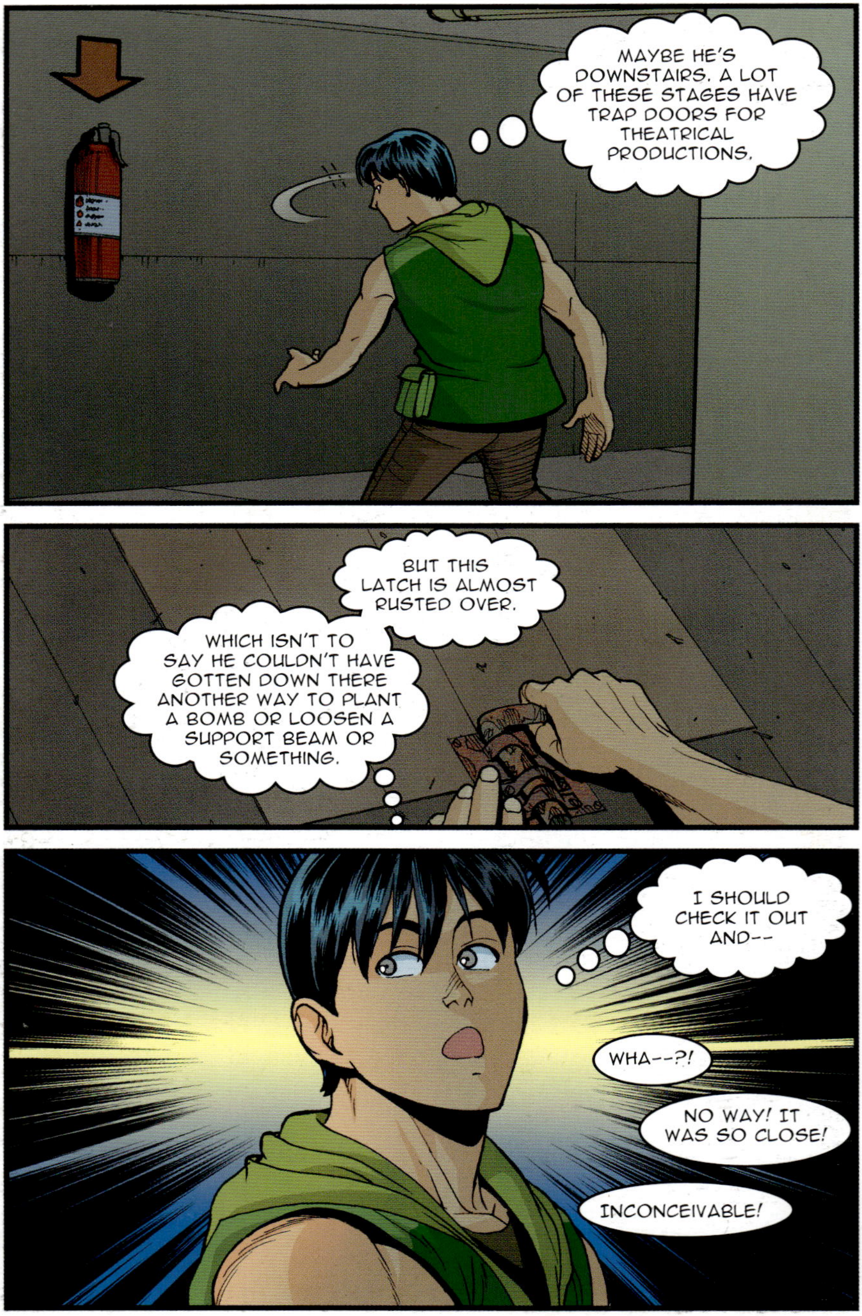
MAYBE HE'S DOWNSTAIRS. A LOT OF THESE STAGES HAVE TRAP DOORS FOR THEATRICAL PRODUCTIONS.
BUT THIS LATCH IS ALMOST RUSTED OVER.
WHICH ISN'T TO SAY HE COULDN'T HAVE GOTTEN DOWN THERE ANOTHER WAY TO PLANT A BOMB OR LOOSEN A SUPPORT BEAM OR SOMETHING.
I SHOULD CHECK IT OUT AND--
WHA--?!
NO WAY! IT WAS SO CLOSE!
INCONCEIVABLE!

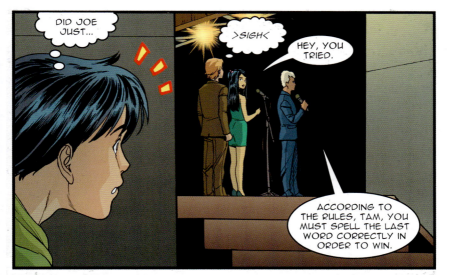

DID JOE JUST...

>SIGH<

HEY, YOU TRIED.

ACCORDING TO THE RULES, TAM, YOU MUST SPELL THE LAST WORD CORRECTLY IN ORDER TO WIN.

I UNDERSTAND, SIR.

MY CELL PHONE.

GLAD I HAD IT ON LOW.

CHRRRRP

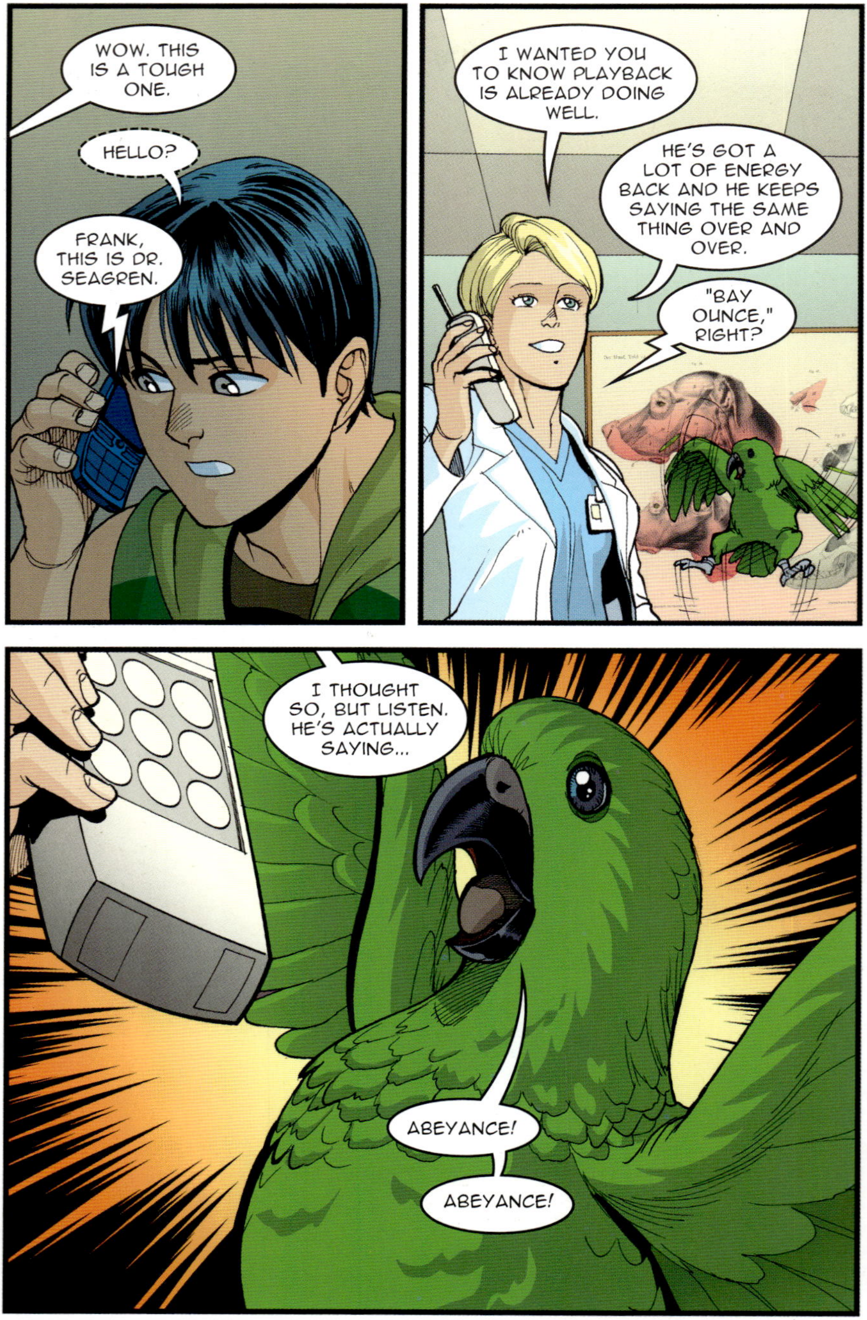
WOW. THIS IS A TOUGH ONE.
HELLO?
FRANK, THIS IS DR. SEAGREN.
I WANTED YOU TO KNOW PLAYBACK IS ALREADY DOING WELL.
HE'S GOT A LOT OF ENERGY BACK AND HE KEEPS SAYING THE SAME THING OVER AND OVER.
"BAY OUNCE," RIGHT?
I THOUGHT SO, BUT LISTEN. HE'S ACTUALLY SAYING...
ABEYANCE!
ABEYANCE!

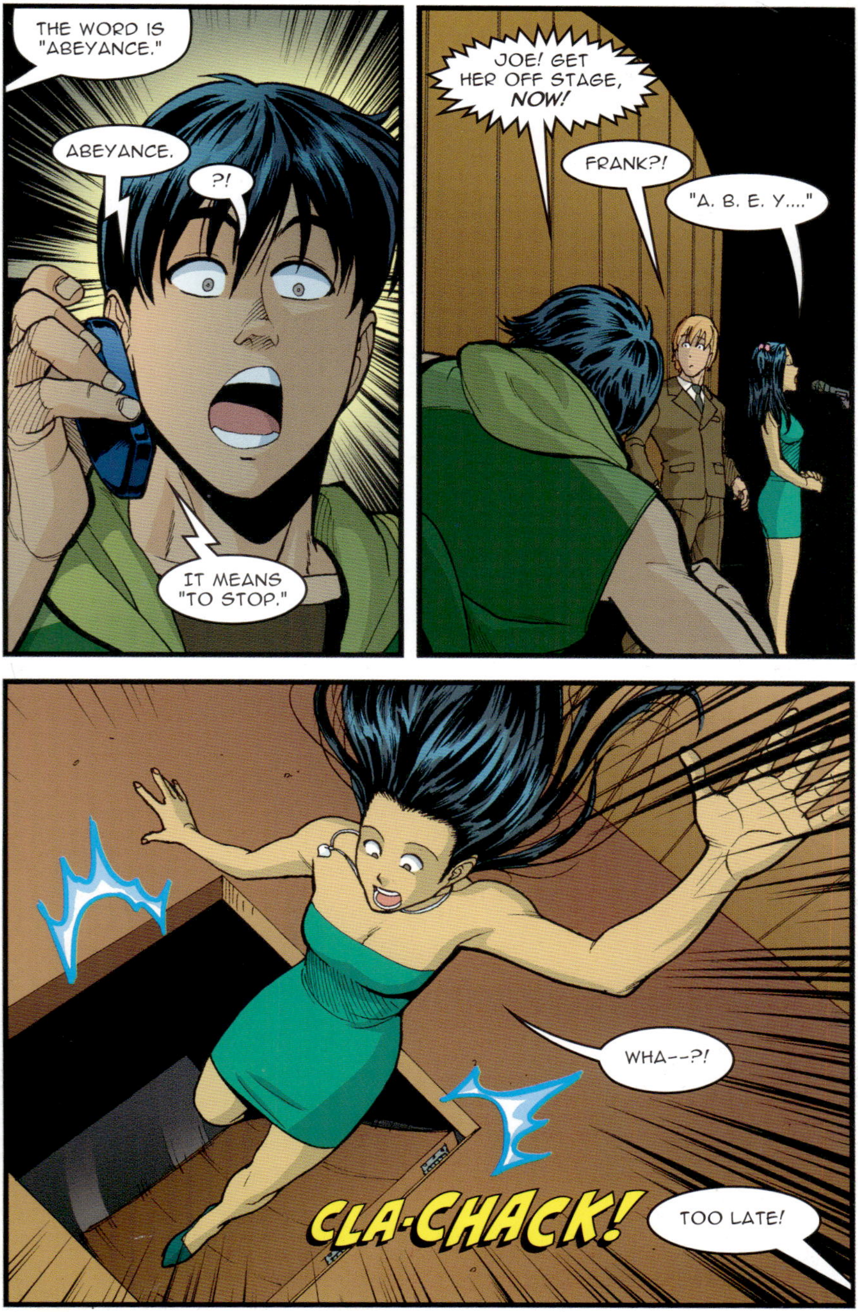
THE WORD IS "ABEYANCE."
ABEYANCE.
?!
IT MEANS "TO STOP."
JOE! GET HER OFF STAGE, NOW!
FRANK?!
"A. B. E. Y...."
WHA--?!
CLA-CHACK!
TOO LATE!

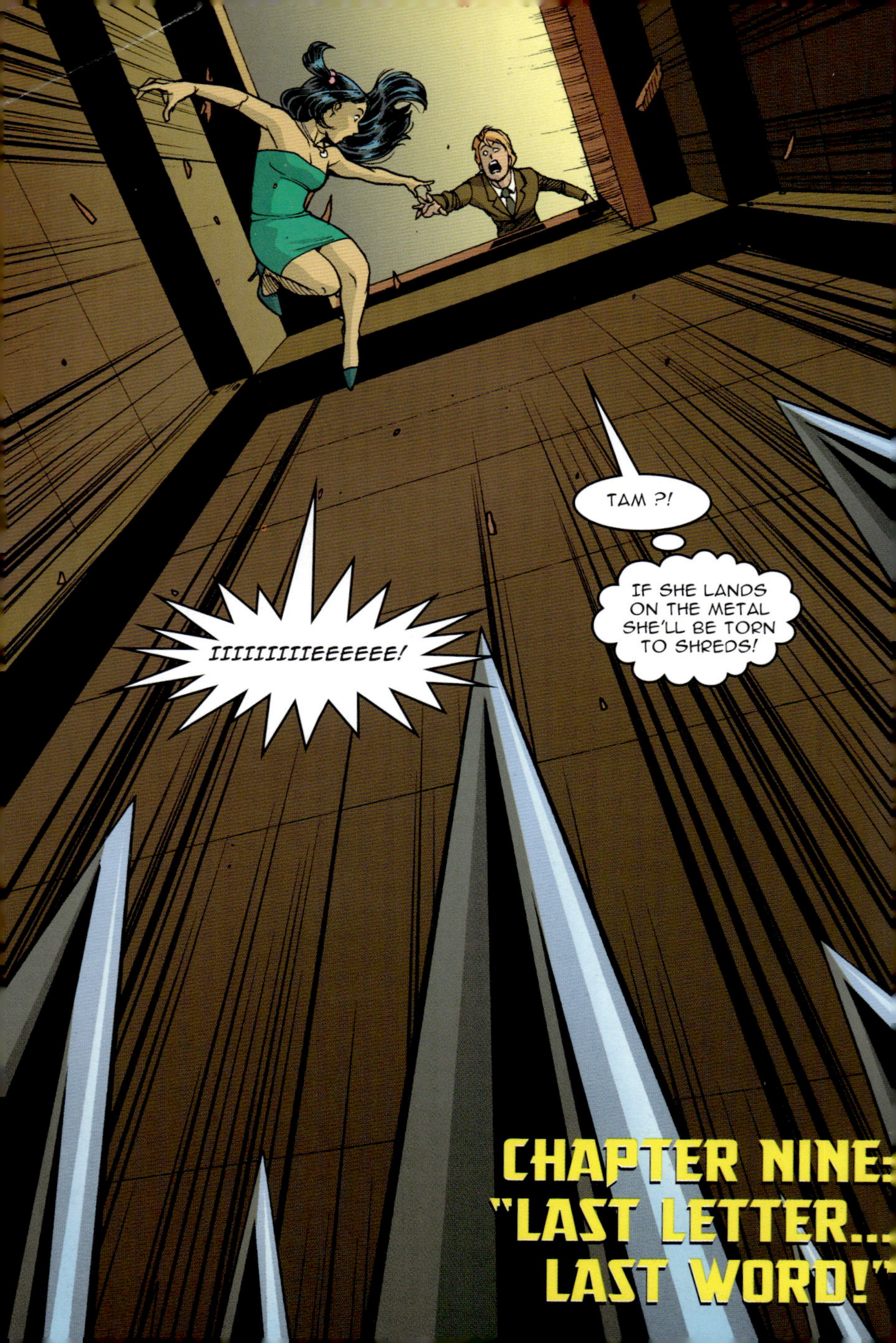
TAM ?!
IF SHE LANDS ON THE METAL SHE'LL BE TORN TO SHREDS!
IIIIIIIIIEEEEEE!
CHAPTER NINE: "LAST LETTER... LAST WORD!"

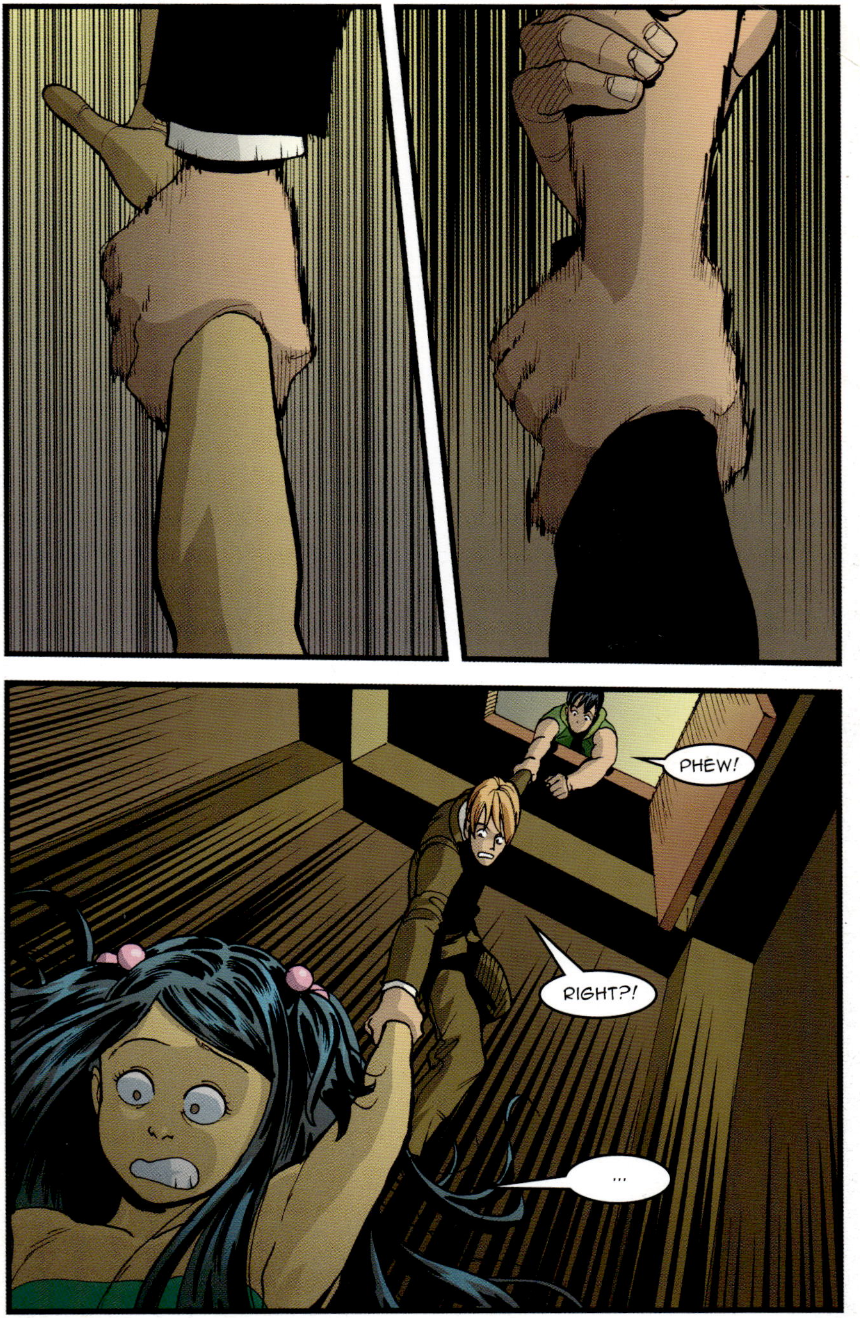
PHEW!
RIGHT?!
...

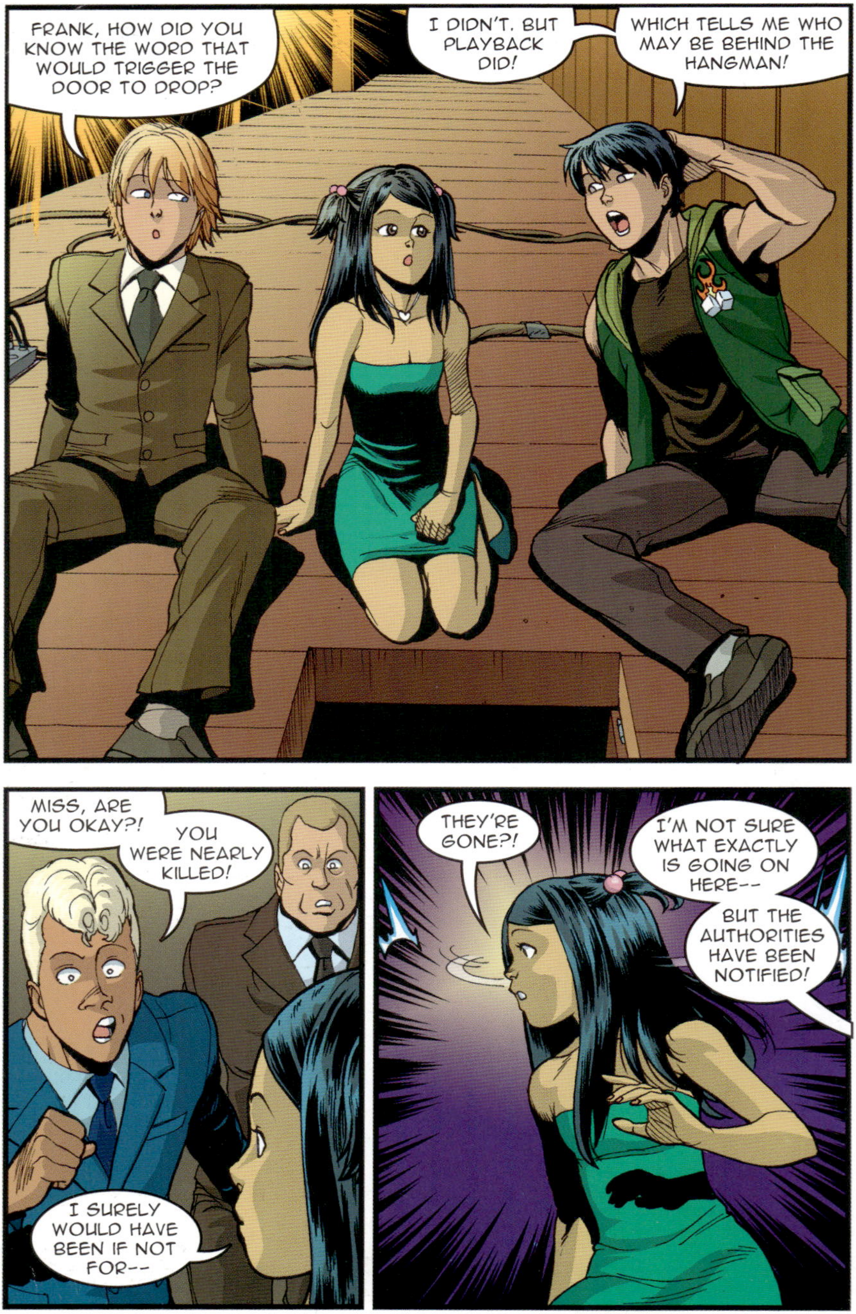
FRANK, HOW DID YOU KNOW THE WORD THAT WOULD TRIGGER THE DOOR TO DROP?
I DIDN'T. BUT PLAYBACK DID!
WHICH TELLS ME WHO MAY BE BEHIND THE HANGMAN!
MISS, ARE YOU OKAY?!
YOU WERE NEARLY KILLED!
I SURELY WOULD HAVE BEEN IF NOT FOR--
THEY'RE GONE?!
I'M NOT SURE WHAT EXACTLY IS GOING ON HERE--
BUT THE AUTHORITIES HAVE BEEN NOTIFIED!

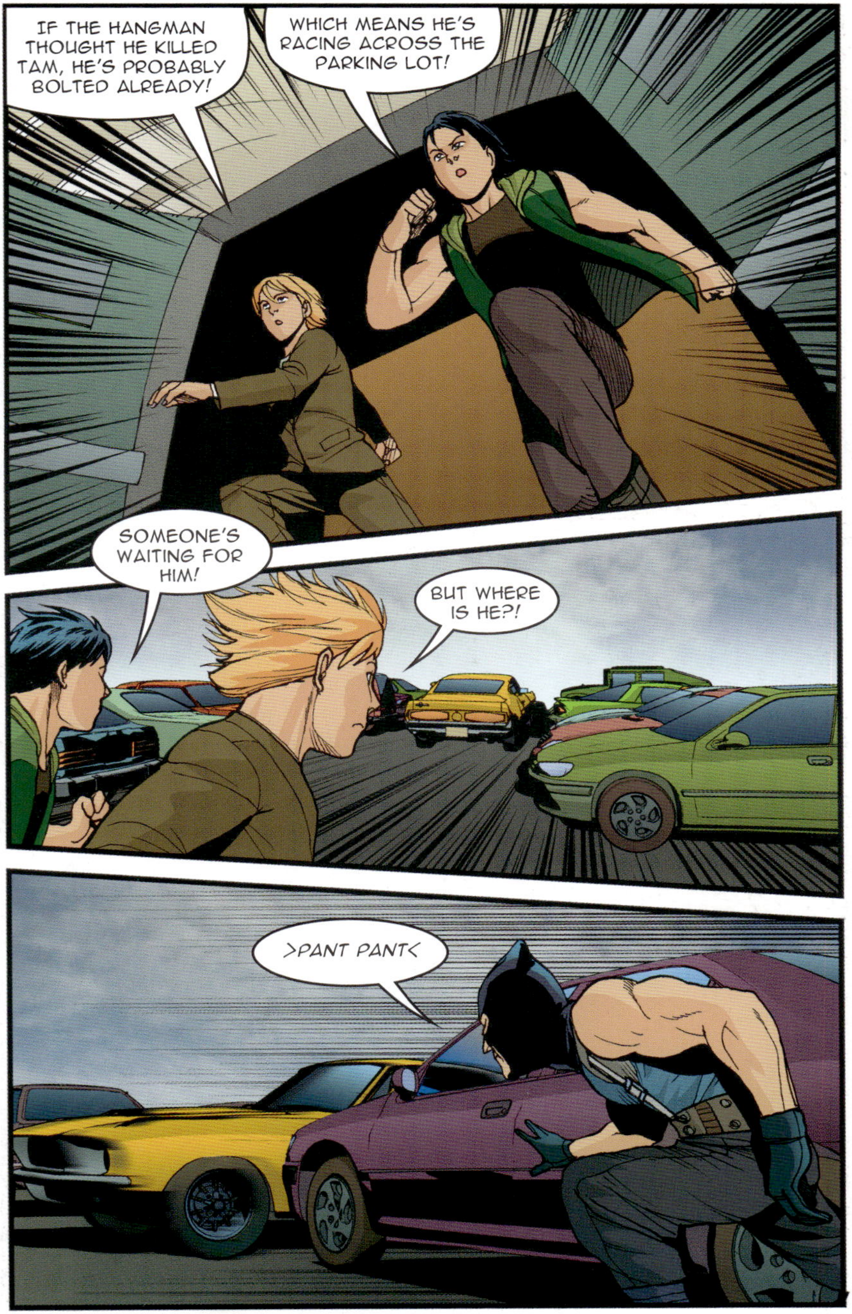
IF THE HANGMAN THOUGHT HE KILLED TAM, HE'S PROBABLY BOLTED ALREADY!
WHICH MEANS HE'S RACING ACROSS THE PARKING LOT!
SOMEONE'S WAITING FOR HIM!
BUT WHERE IS HE?!
>PANT PANT<

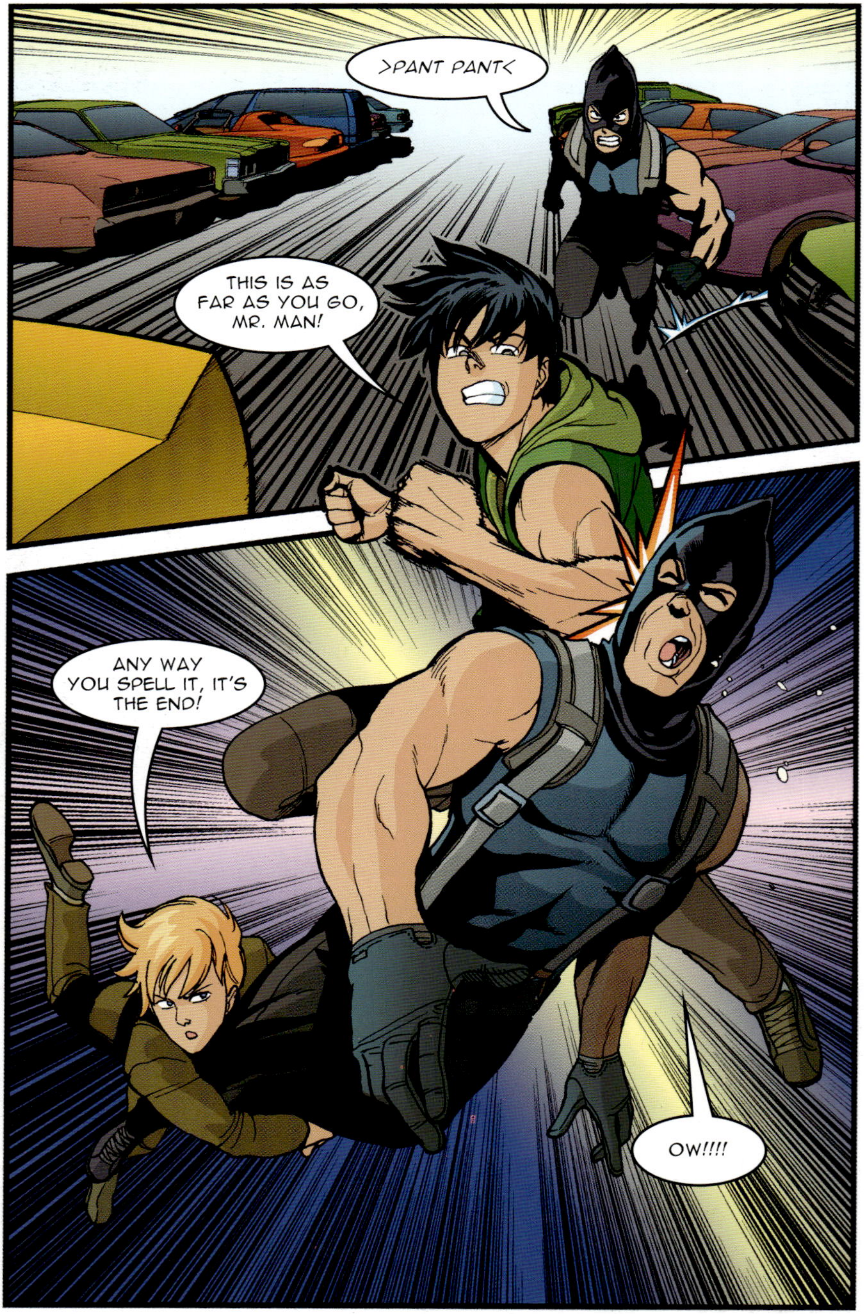
>PANT PANT<
THIS IS AS FAR AS YOU GO, MR. MAN!
ANY WAY YOU SPELL IT, IT'S THE END!
OW!!!!

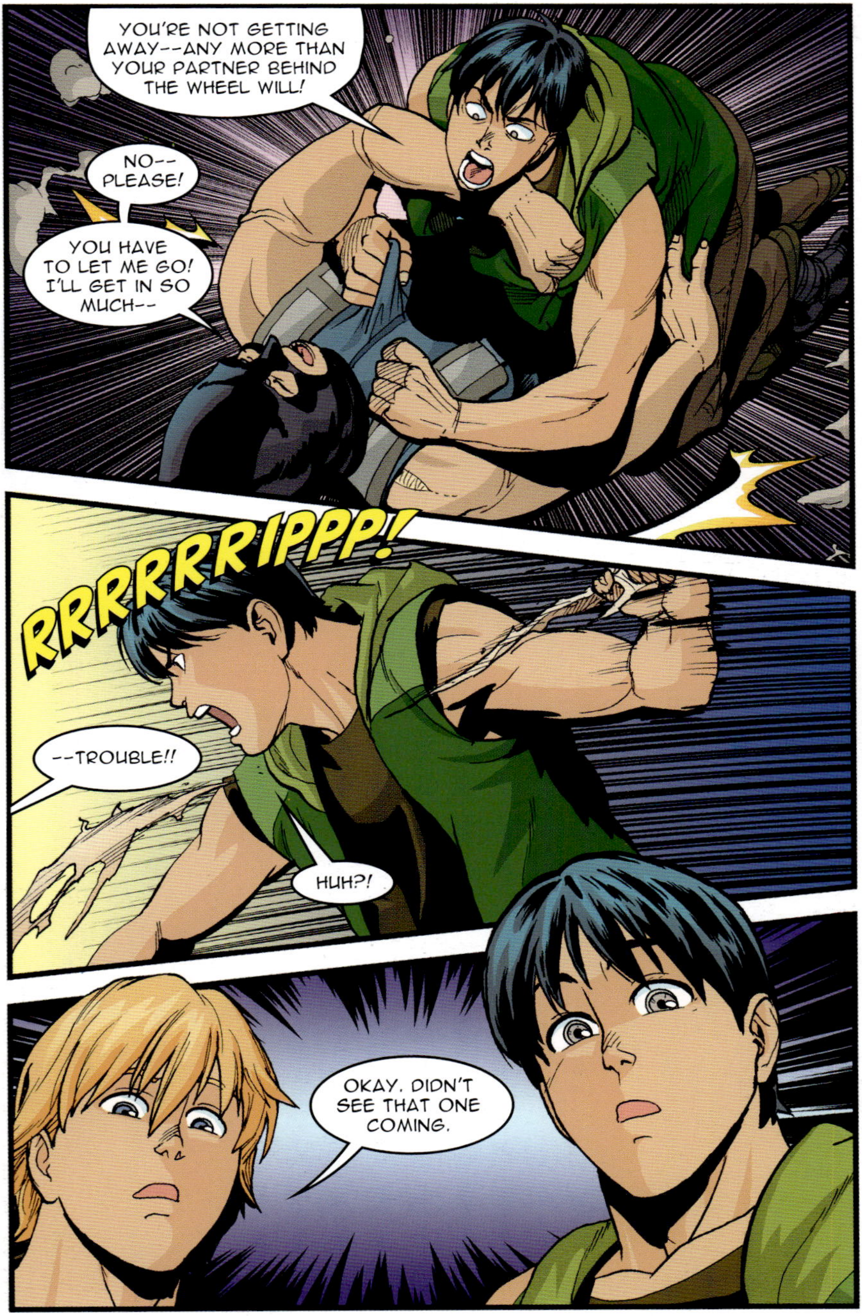
YOU'RE NOT GETTING AWAY--ANY MORE THAN YOUR PARTNER BEHIND THE WHEEL WILL!
NO-- PLEASE!
YOU HAVE TO LET ME GO! I'LL GET IN SO MUCH--
RRRRRRIPPP!
--TROUBLE!!
HUH?!
OKAY. DIDN'T SEE THAT ONE COMING.

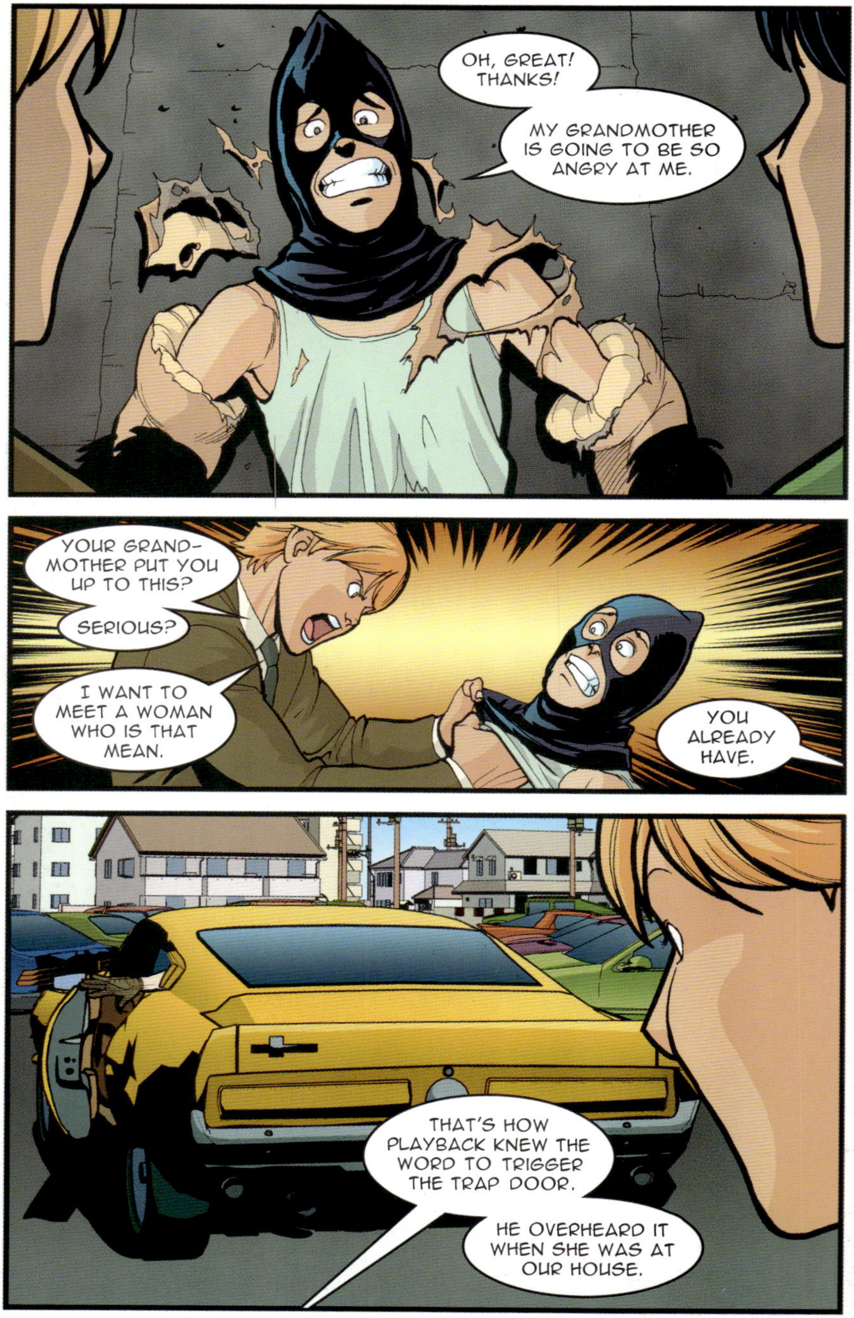

OH, GREAT! THANKS!
MY GRANDMOTHER IS GOING TO BE SO ANGRY AT ME.
YOUR GRAND-MOTHER PUT YOU UP TO THIS?
SERIOUS?
I WANT TO MEET A WOMAN WHO IS THAT MEAN.
YOU ALREADY HAVE.
THAT'S HOW PLAYBACK KNEW THE WORD TO TRIGGER THE TRAP DOOR.
HE OVERHEARD IT WHEN SHE WAS AT OUR HOUSE.

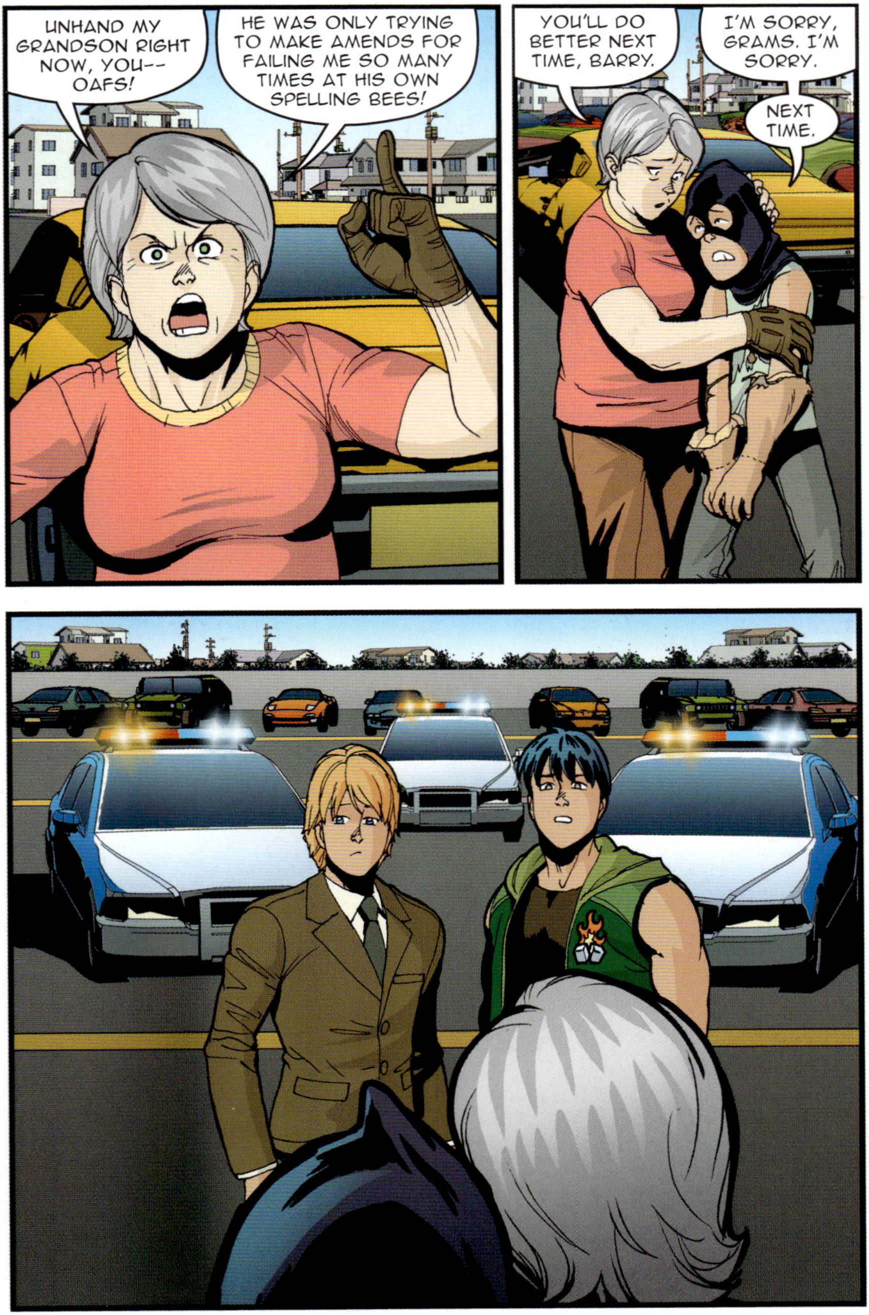
UNHAND MY GRANDSON RIGHT NOW, YOU-- OAFS!
HE WAS ONLY TRYING TO MAKE AMENDS FOR FAILING ME SO MANY TIMES AT HIS OWN SPELLING BEES!
YOU'LL DO BETTER NEXT TIME, BARRY.
I'M SORRY, GRAMS. I'M SORRY.
NEXT TIME.

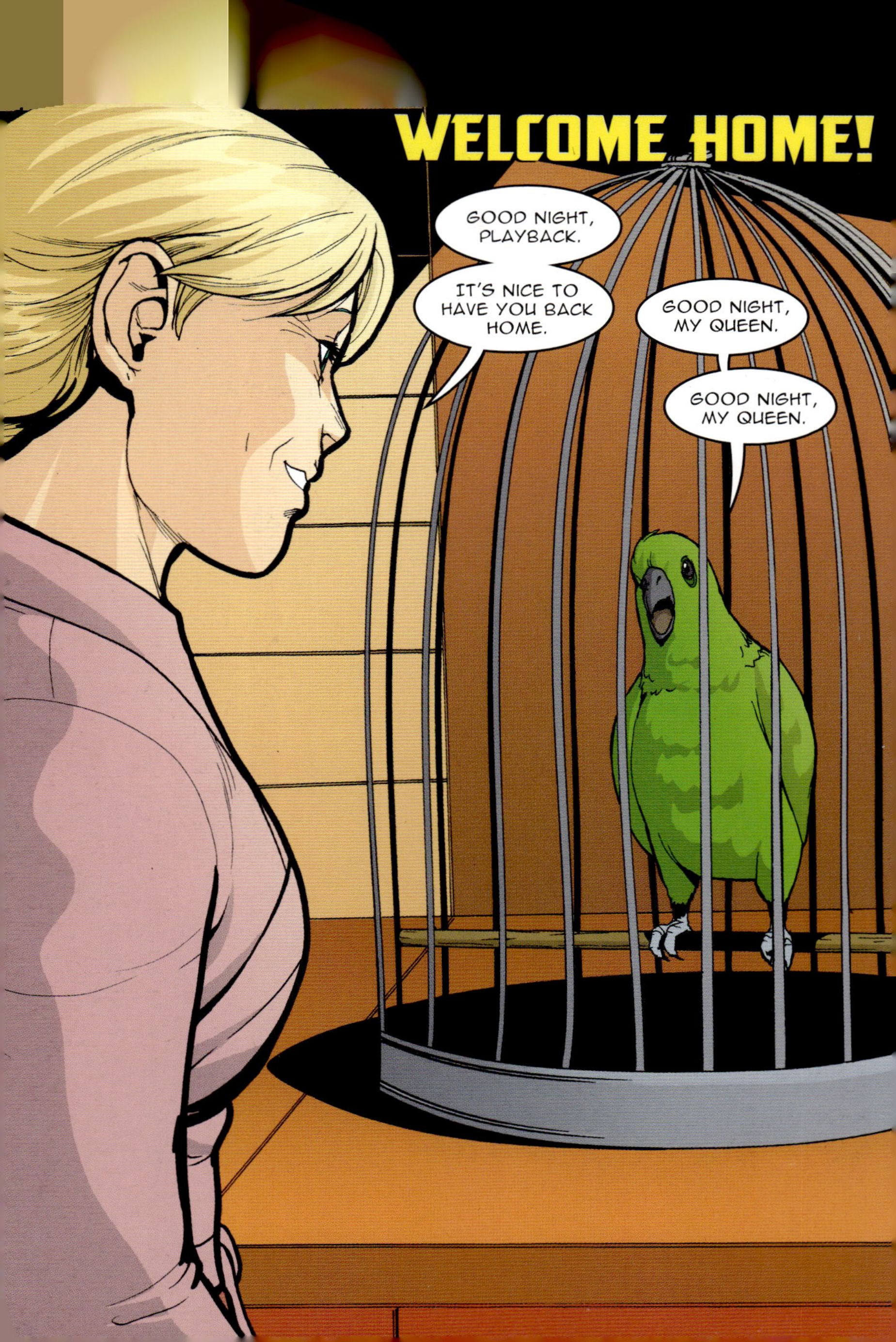
WELCOME HOME!
GOOD NIGHT, PLAYBACK.
IT'S NICE TO HAVE YOU BACK HOME.
GOOD NIGHT, MY QUEEN.
GOOD NIGHT, MY QUEEN.

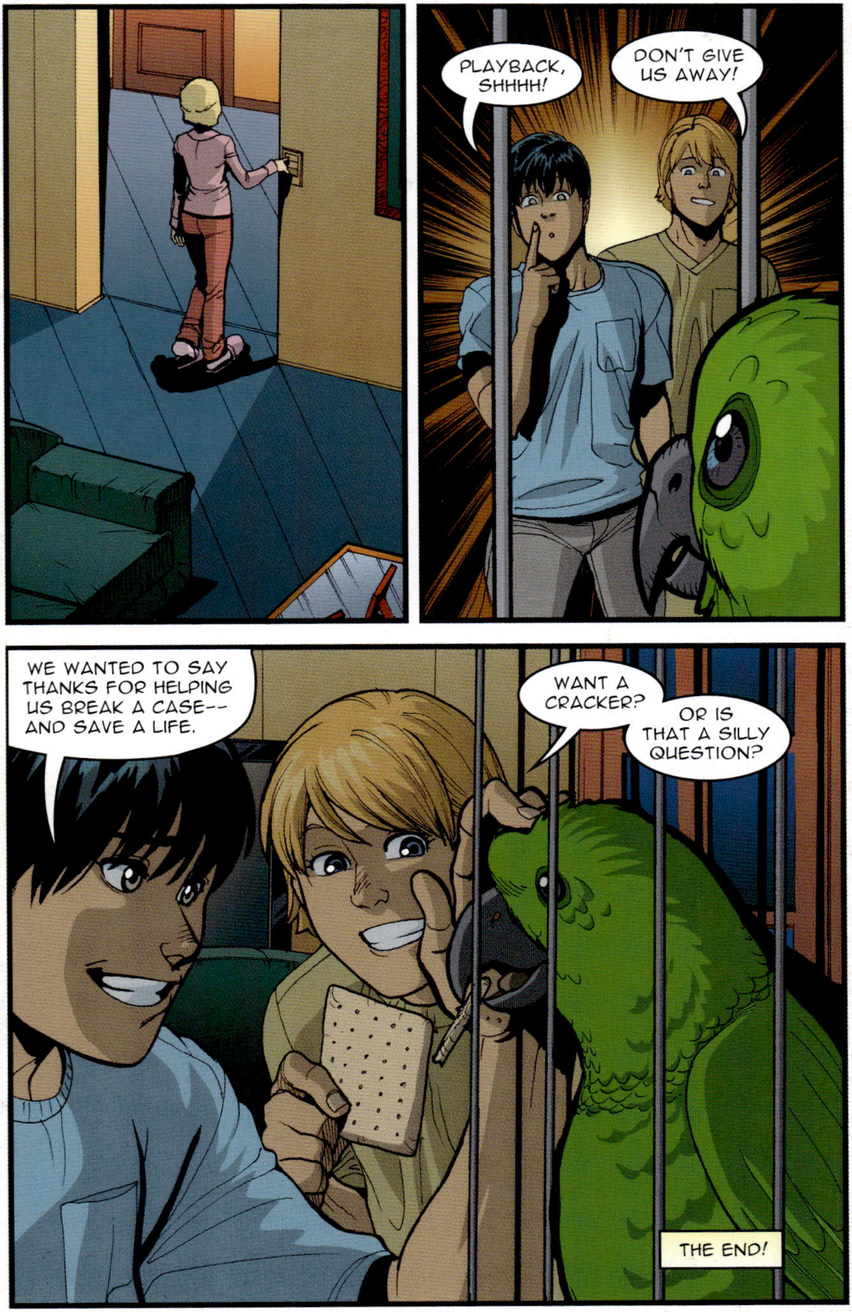
PLAYBACK, SHHHH!
DON'T GIVE US AWAY!
WE WANTED TO SAY THANKS FOR HELPING US BREAK A CASE-- AND SAVE A LIFE.
WANT A CRACKER?
OR IS THAT A SILLY QUESTION?
THE END!

NANCY DREW

A NEW GRAPHIC NOVEL EVERY 3 MONTHS!

#13 – "Doggone Town"
ISBN – 978-1-59707-098-0
#14 – "Sleight of Dan"
ISBN – 978-1-59707-107-9
#15 – "Tiger Counter"
ISBN – 978-1-59707-118-5
#16 – "What Goes Up..."
ISBN – 978-1-59707-134-5
NEW! #17 – "Night of the Living Chatchke"
ISBN - 978-1-59707-143-7

NEW STORY! FULL-COLOR GRAPHIC NOVEL
NANCY DREW
girl detective
#17
NIGHT OF THE LIVING CHATCHKE
BASED ON THE SERIES BY CAROLYN KEENE
"The Secret Within" Book One
PETRUCHA
KINNEY
MURASE
GUZMAN
PAPERCUTZ

Also available – Nancy Drew #1-12
All: Pocket-sized, 96-112 pp., full-color $7.95
Also available in hardcover for $12.95 each

NANCY DREW
Graphic Novels #1-4 Boxed Set
ISBN – 978-1-59707-038-6
NANCY DREW
Graphic Novels #5-8 Boxed Set
ISBN – 978-1-59707-074-4
NANCY DREW
Graphic Novels #9-12 Boxed Set
ISBN – 978-1-59707-126-0

NANCY DREW
PAPERCUTZ

CLASSICS *Illustrated* Deluxe

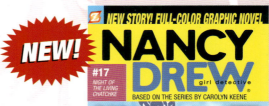

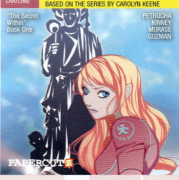

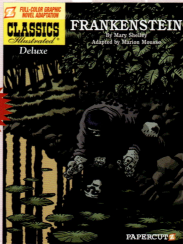

#1 "The Wind in the Willows"
ISBN – 978-159707-096-6
#2 "Tales from the Brothers Grimm"
ISBN – 978-159707-100-0
NEW! #3 "Frankenstein"
ISBN – 978-159707-131-4
All: 6 1/2 x 9, 144 pp. full-color, $13.95
Also available in hardcover for $17.95 each

FULL-COLOR GRAPHIC NOVEL ADAPTATION
CLASSICS Illustrated
Deluxe
FRANKENSTEIN
By Mary Shelley
Adapted by Marion Mousse
PAPERCUTZ

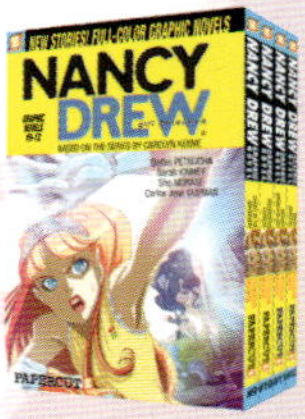

ON SALE AT BOOKSELLERS EVERYWHERE!

Please add $4.00 postage and handling. Add $1.00 for each additional item.
Make check payable to NBM publishing. Send to:
Papercutz, 40 Exchange Place, Suite 1308,
New York, New York 10005, 1-800-886-1223

www.papercutz.com

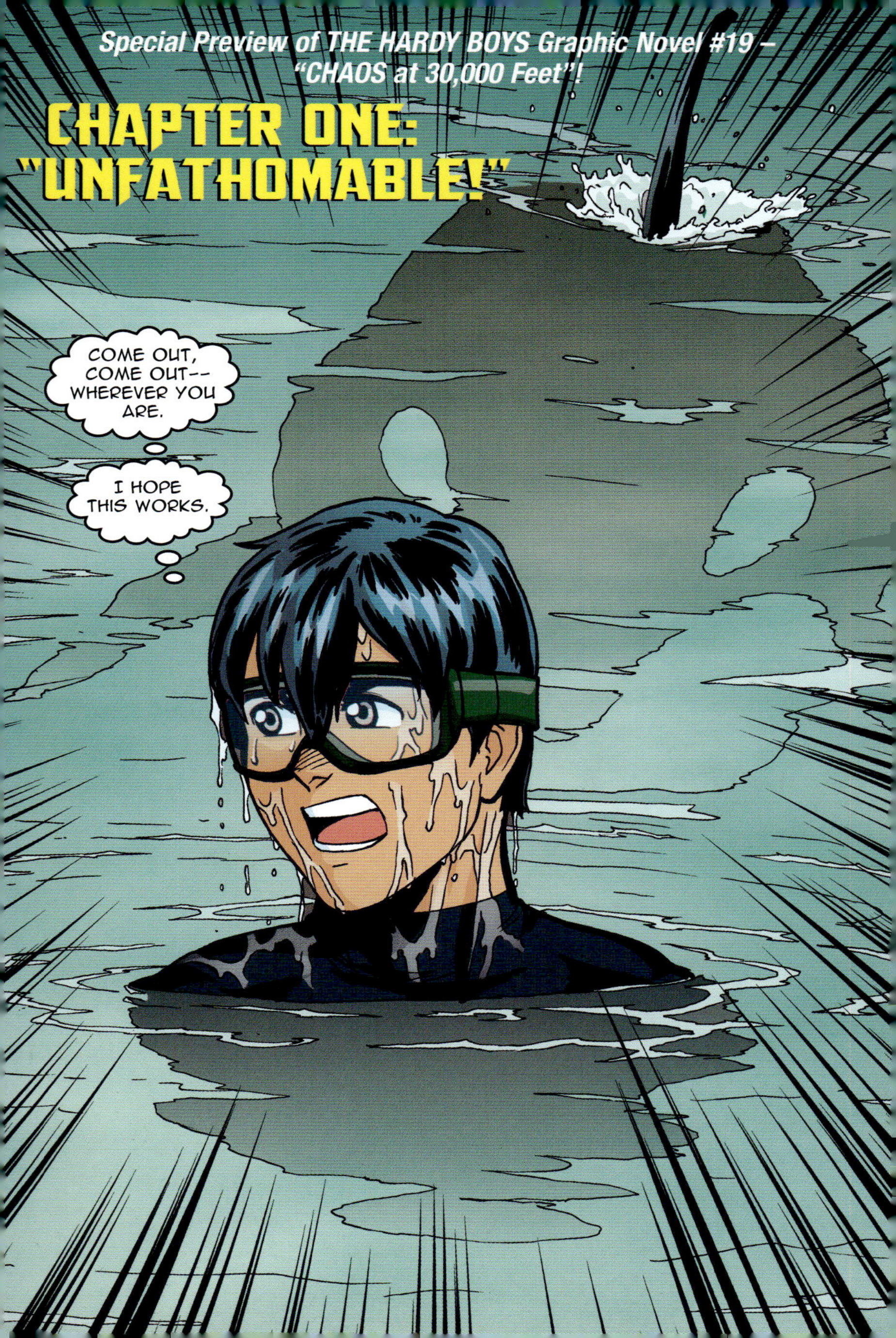
Special Preview of THE HARDY BOYS Graphic Novel #19 – "CHAOS at 30,000 Feet"!
CHAPTER ONE: "UNFATHOMABLE!"
COME OUT, COME OUT-- WHEREVER YOU ARE.
I HOPE THIS WORKS.

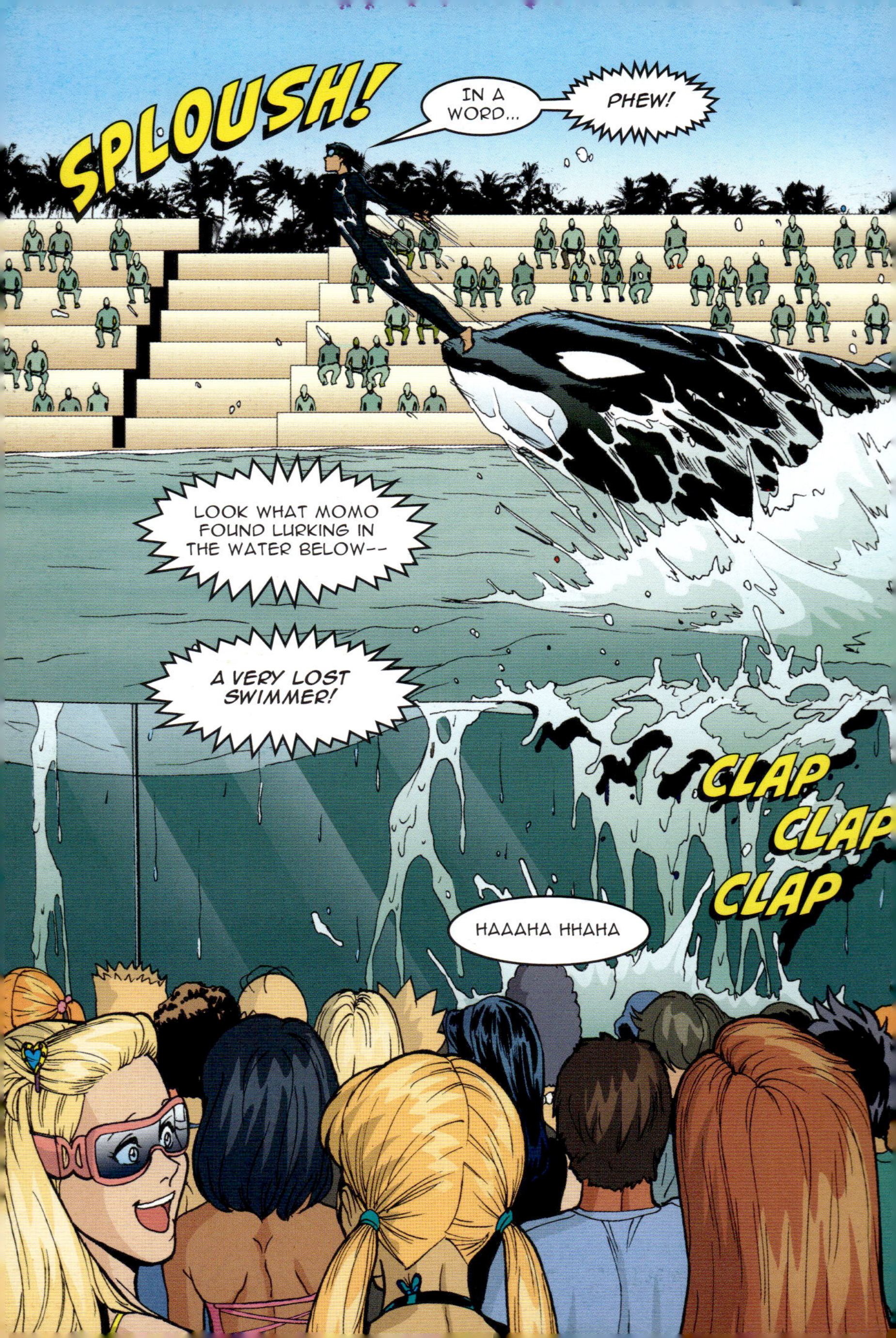
SPLOUSH!
IN A WORD...
PHEW!
LOOK WHAT MOMO FOUND LURKING IN THE WATER BELOW--
A VERY LOST SWIMMER!
CLAP
CLAP
CLAP
HAAAHA HHAHA

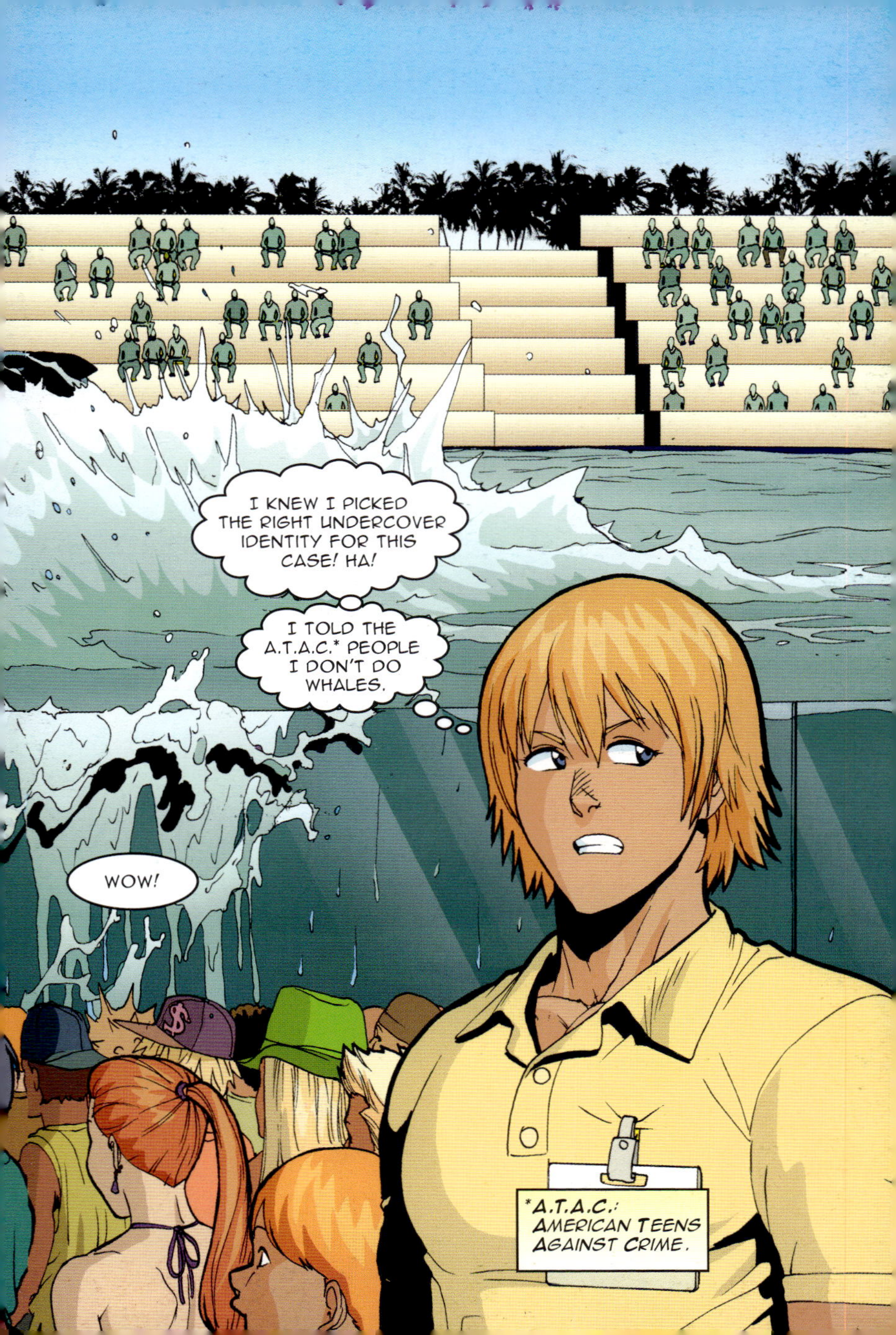
I KNEW I PICKED THE RIGHT UNDERCOVER IDENTITY FOR THIS CASE! HA!
I TOLD THE A.T.A.C.* PEOPLE I DON'T DO WHALES.
WOW!
*A.T.A.C.: AMERICAN TEENS AGAINST CRIME.

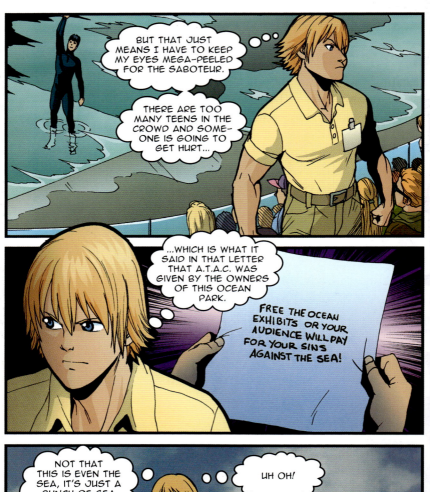

BUT THAT JUST MEANS I HAVE TO KEEP MY EYES MEGA-PEELED FOR THE SABOTEUR.

THERE ARE TOO MANY TEENS IN THE CROWD AND SOMEONE IS GOING TO GET HURT...

...WHICH IS WHAT IT SAID IN THAT LETTER THAT A.T.A.C. WAS GIVEN BY THE OWNERS OF THIS OCEAN PARK.

FREE THE OCEAN EXHIBITS OR YOUR AUDIENCE WILL PAY FOR YOUR SINS AGAINST THE SEA!

NOT THAT THIS IS EVEN THE SEA, IT'S JUST A BUNCH OF SEA WATER IN TANKS AND --

UH OH!

Don't Miss THE HARDY BOYS Graphic Novel #19 - "CHAOS at 30,000 Feet!"

WATCH OUT FOR PAPERCUTZ™

For long-time followers of THE HARDY BOYS Graphic Novels, I don't need to tell you that this little section of the book is called the Papercutz Backpages – the place to find out all sorts of things about all your favorite Papercutz titles and creators. But if this particular HARDY BOYS Graphic Novel is your very first Papercutz experience, then welcome! I'm Jim Salicrup, the lucky guy who happens to be the Editor-in-Chief of this wonderful little comics and graphic novels–creating company.

Not only do we bring you all-new exciting HARDY BOYS graphic novels every three months, but we also publish all-new graphic novels starring NANCY DREW, BIONICLE, and TALES FROM THE CRYPT. We also bring you comics adaptations of Stories by the World's Greatest Authors in CLASSICS ILLUSTRATED and CLASSICS ILLUSTRATED DELUXE. We also have a new series of graphic novels starring a time-traveling mouse named GERONIMO STILTON, who is saving the future, by protecting the past. We have another all-new series coming your way, but let's keep that a secret for just a little longer.

Of course, the very best way to get the most up-to-date Papercutz news and information is to visit our website at www.papercutz.com. Perhaps the most popular feature on there is our Papercutz Blog, featuring posts by such Papercutz super-stars as Scott Lobdell, Paulo Henrique, Stefan Petrucha, Sarah Kinney, Sho Murase, Greg Farshtey, and Michael Petranek! The stuff on the Blog is so great, we'll be running some of the best bits here as well. For example, the Papercutz Profile on THE HARDY BOYS artist Paulo Henrique (or "PH" as he prefers) originally appeared online, but we added some more art and photos, and are running it at the end of this edition of the Papercutz Backpages.

But that's not all! We also have a special preview of perhaps the most eagerly awaited edition of TALES FROM THE CRYPT -- #8 "Diary of a Stinky Dead Kid." We think the cover may give you a clue why…

To get just a small sample of what all the fuss is about, check out the preview on the next few pages!

So, enjoy the Paulo profile, the Papercutz Blog, and the CRYPT preview – and don't forget, we'll be back soon in HARDY BOYS Graphic Novel #19 when you'll need to buckle your safety belt to survive "Chaos at 30,000 Feet!"

Thanks,

Jim

TALES FROM THE CRYPT
PRESENTS
DIARY of a Stinky Dead Kid
All-New Stories!
Full-Color Graphic Novel
PAPERCUTZ

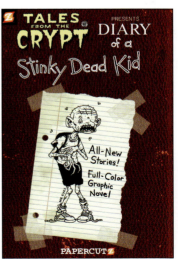

Here's a preview of TALES FROM THE CRYPT # 8 "Diary of a Stinky Dead Kid"
by Stefan Petrucha and Rick Parker…

October
Monday

My name's Glugg. It's always sad and scary when a kid dies, especially if it's you. Funny, for the longest time I thought the scariest thing was my brother, Rock.

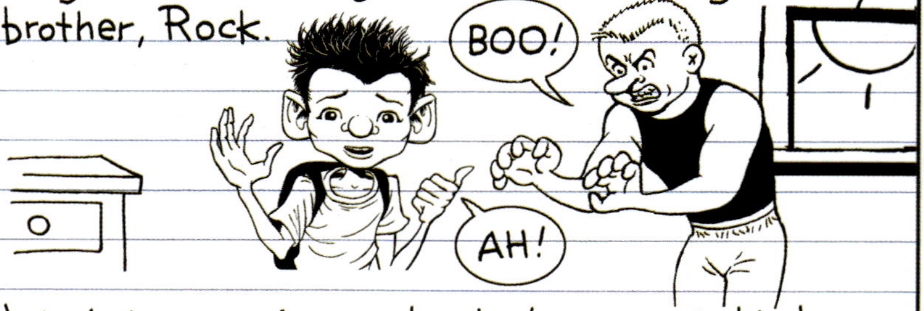
BOO!
AH!

He's twice my size and only has room in his brain for his band, bullying me and making fun of this journal. I think he's jealous I can write. Plus he wants a new drum set badly, and our parents made it clear we can't afford one.

Anyway, it turns out there ARE things scarier than Rock, just a couple, though, like death.

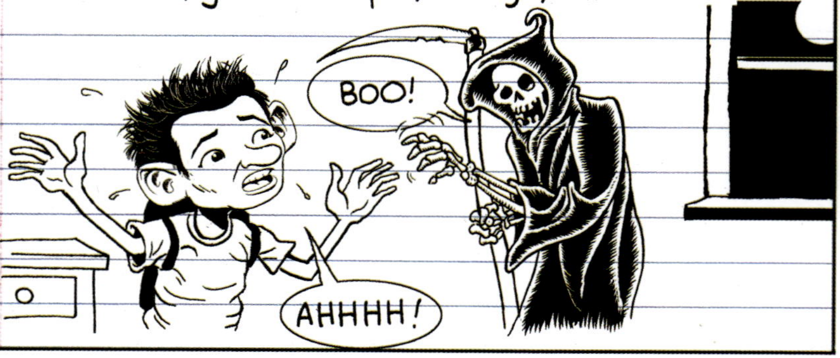
BOO!
AHHHH!

Have you ever just KNOWN the phone will ring and exactly who's calling and you feel really cool, like it's magic or something?

You'd think with something big as DEATH, you'd get the same kind of warning, but nope. Not me, anyway. No bells, no whistles, not even a vague sense of impending doom.

It sucks! I mean I was minding my own business, standing next to my pal Al Crowley at the train station with the rest of the kids, on our dumb school trip to the Museum, when...

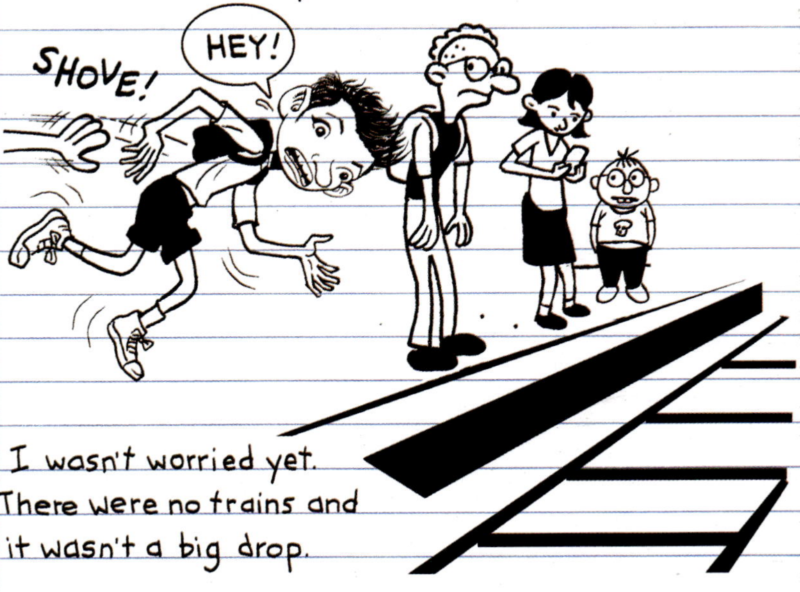

SHOVE!
HEY!

I wasn't worried yet.
There were no trains and it wasn't a big drop.

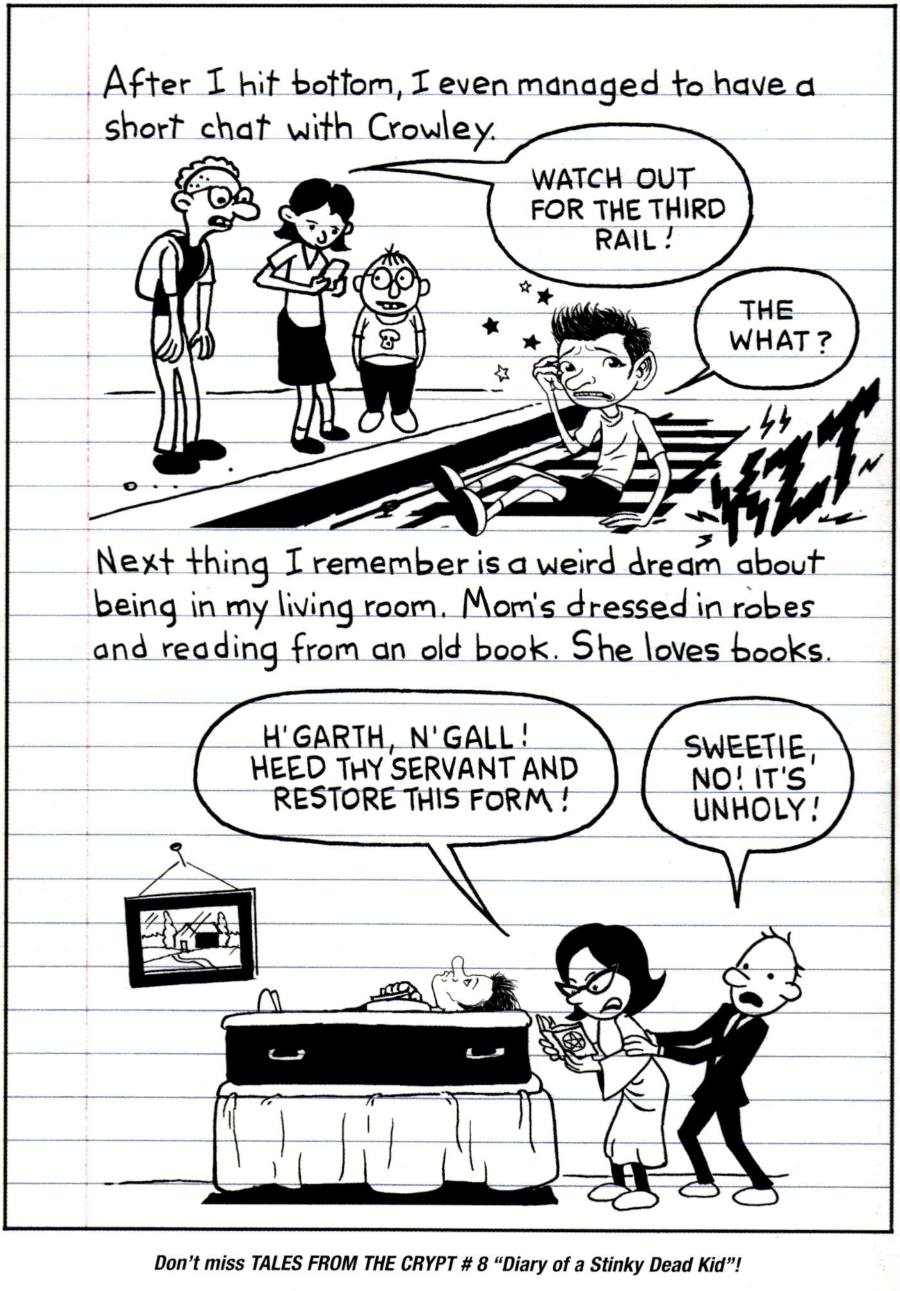
After I hit bottom, I even managed to have a short chat with Crowley.
WATCH OUT FOR THE THIRD RAIL!
THE WHAT?
Next thing I remember is a weird dream about being in my living room. Mom's dressed in robes and reading from an old book. She loves books.
H'GARTH, N'GALL! HEED THY SERVANT AND RESTORE THIS FORM!
SWEETIE, NO! IT'S UNHOLY!

Don't miss TALES FROM THE CRYPT # 8 "Diary of a Stinky Dead Kid"!

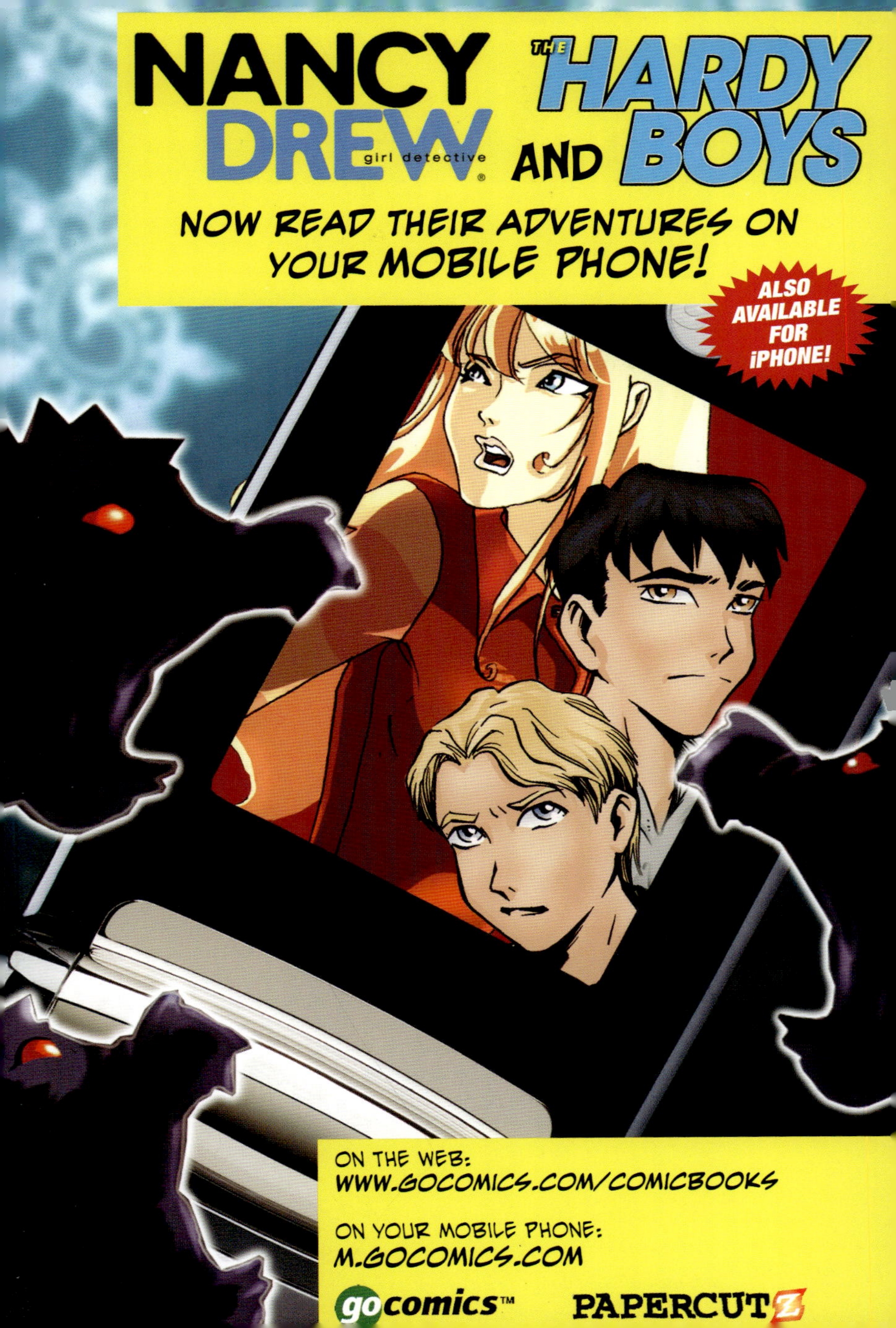

NANCY DREW girl detective®
AND
THE HARDY BOYS
NOW READ THEIR ADVENTURES ON YOUR MOBILE PHONE!
ALSO AVAILABLE FOR iPHONE!
ON THE WEB:
WWW.GOCOMICS.COM/COMICBOOKS
ON YOUR MOBILE PHONE:
M.GOCOMICS.COM
gocomics™
PAPERCUTZ

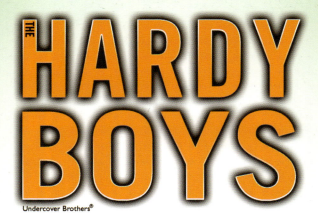

THE HARDY BOYS

Undercover Brothers®

New reality show Deprivation House is supposed to show how long contestants can survive without modern luxuries.

Trouble is, some of the contestants aren't surviving at all.

Catch undercover agents Frank and Joe Hardy in the new Murder House trilogy!

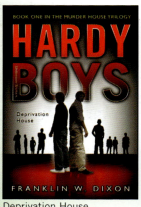

Deprivation House

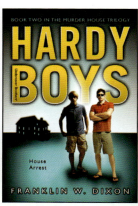

House Arrest

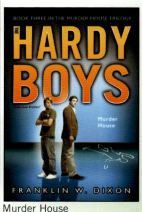

Murder House

Available wherever books are sold

 ALADDIN • SIMON & SCHUSTER CHILDREN'S PUBLISHING • SIMONSAYSKIDS.COM

MEET HARDY BOYS GRAPHIC NOVELS ARTIST "PH"-

PAULO HENRIQUE!

A PAPERCUTZ PROFILE

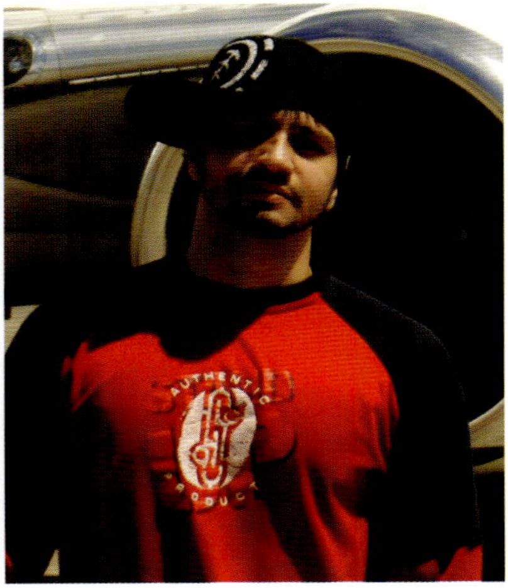
AUTHENTIC
PRODUCT

Hi there, my name is Paulo Henrique and most of you know me as the artist of THE HARDY BOYS Graphic Novels for Papercutz. One thing you might not know is that I prefer to go by "PH" instead of "Paulo Henrique." I'd like to share a bit about myself and let you all ask any questions you may have for me over on the Papercutz Blog (go to www.papercutz.com). I always like to hear from fans.

I was born in Sao Paulo, Brazil where I started drawing at a very young age. The first thing I remember drawing was from when I was 6 years old. I was in art class and I drew a picture of Darth Vader – the villain from STAR WARS. The teacher said she thought that I had drawn a bride in a black wedding dress! I always liked bad guys the best, but I knew that Vader was a good guy under that mask. That's why I liked him so much as a kid.

After that, I just kept on drawing and drawing. I really like "larger than life" characters, and when I was growing up I was drawn to Manga-style art before I even knew that's what it was called. Manga is actually the Japanese word for comics, but there are many unique elements of this Japanese art style that we use in THE HARDY BOYS a lot. An easy way to identify the style is characters with cartoonishly exaggerated faces and bodies. If you want a good example of some Manga-esque HARDY BOYS, look at the fourth page of comics in THE HARDY BOYS Graphic Novel #14 "Haley Danielle's Top Eight!":

Some of the best-known artists who shaped what we know as Manga today are Machiko Hasegawa and Osamu Tezuka. You have probably seen Tezuka's "Astro Boy" at some point in your life. Google it! The history of Manga goes all the way back to the 1800's and there's a lot of info on the Internet if you do some searching.

Back to my art! Some of you may want to know who my favorite comics characters are and how I got started. Well, I love that Blue Bomber! I'm talking about Megaman.

I started drawing him when I was a teenager and I've beaten all of the original Nintendo games. Megaman is a Manga character and he jump-started my career. In 1997, I was hired to draw the MEGAMAN comicbook for Brazilian publisher Magnum and ended up working with Sidney Lima, who would work on ZORRO and THE HARDY BOYS at Papercutz years later. At that time, a lot of publishers got interested in Manga, so I met with Magnum and did a test for Megaman. Both Sidney Lima and I ended up getting the job, and we became friends.

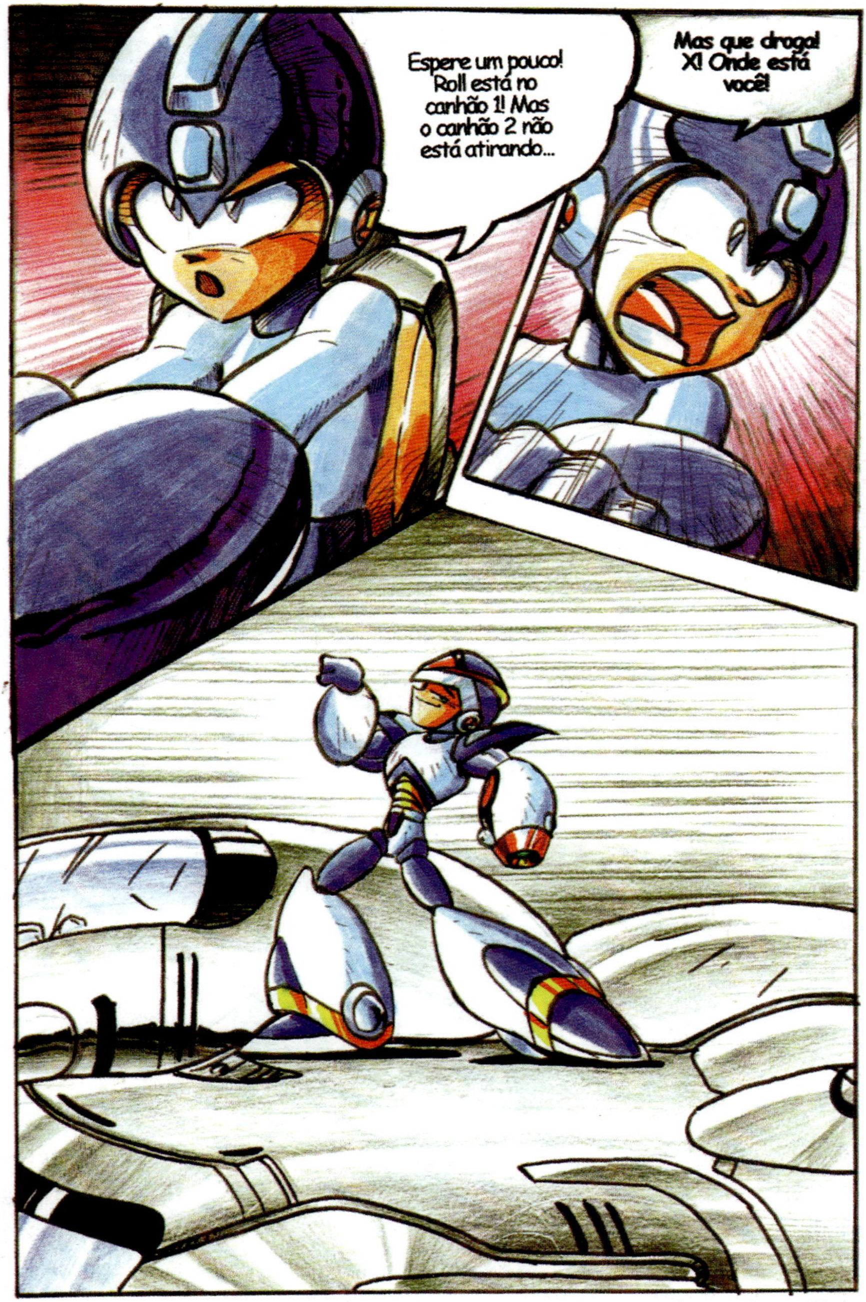
Espere um pouco! Roll está no canhão 1! Mas o canhão 2 não está atirando...
Mas que droga! X! Onde está você!

Years later I started to work for Yabu Media and was doing an electronic graphic novel called COMBO RANGERS, so I called him to work with me. This led to us collaborating on THE HARDY BOYS. He is a good friend and a great artist. I have to thank him for introducing me to Papercutz and THE HARDY BOYS. The MEGAMAN series took off, and I ended up teaching Manga-style drawing to young artists at a place called Impacto Studios in Brazil.

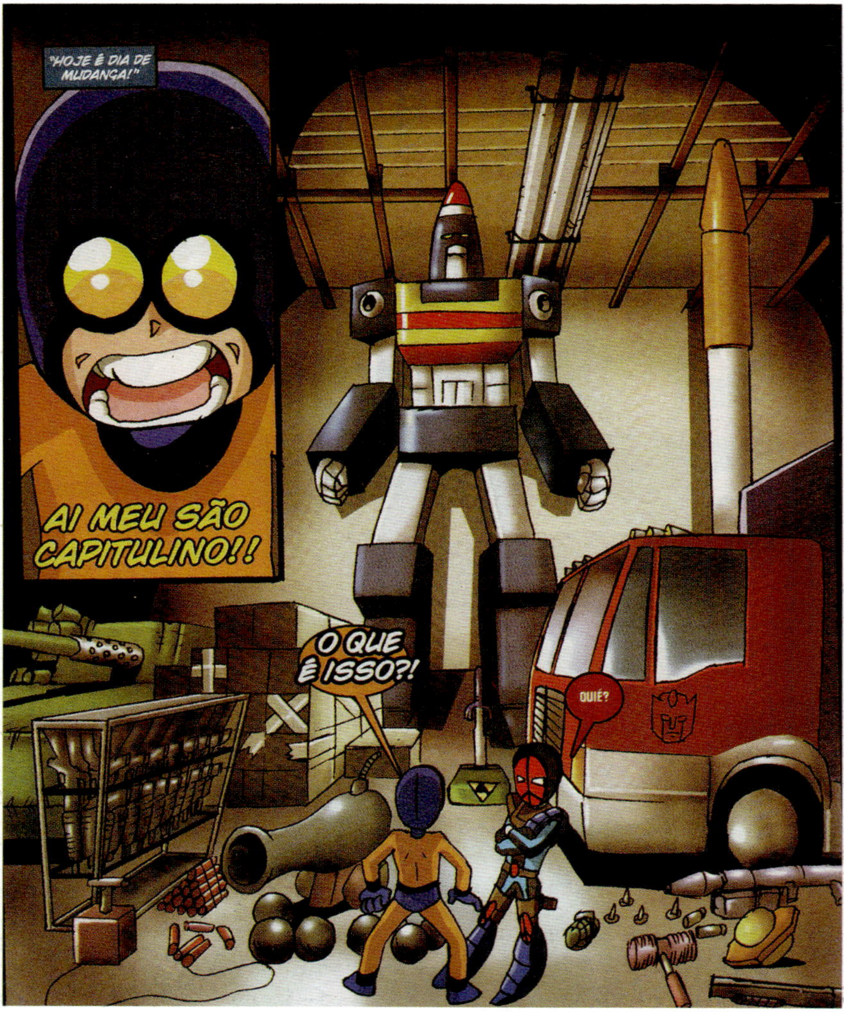
"HOJE É DIA DE MUDANÇA!"
AI MEU SÃO CAPITULINO!!
O QUE É ISSO?!
QUIÉ?

Impacto Studios is a place where young artists can come to learn and improve their art, while more established artists teach classes to students and are introduced to companies that may want to hire them. At Impacto, I became friends with Klebs Junior, the founder of the studio and a comicbook artist himself. Klebs is well-known in comics. Aside from founding Impacto he also illustrated SNAKES ON A PLANE (DC), EXCALIBUR (Marvel Comics), HARBINGER and a bunch of other titles. Klebs became my agent and helped get my work to America. When he heard that Top Cow Productions at Image Comics was looking for an artist for their MYTH WARRIORS series, he set up a test for me. Top Cow hired me and my work ended up getting distributed to a much larger audience in the US.

I worked for a lot of different magazines and publications in Brazil, but it wasn't until THE HARDY BOYS #6 "Hyde and Shriek" that I started working on that series. My friend Sidney needed some help. He asked me to help draw THE HARDY BOYS #6 and then I started drawing it full-time and have no plans to stop! I just finished my 12th volume of the series.

Aside from comics, I really love music. I have remixed a lot of Megaman songs from the

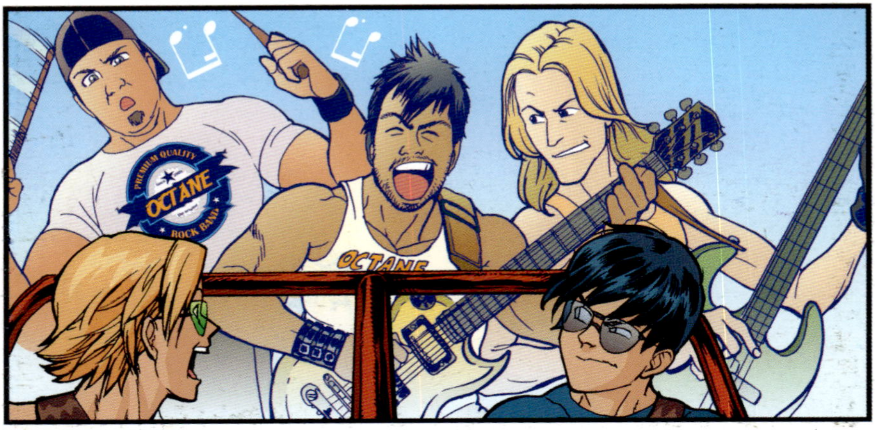

OCTANE
PREMIUM QUALITY
ROCK BAND
OCTANE

Paulo and his band "Octane" in THE HARDY BOYS 17 "Word Up!"

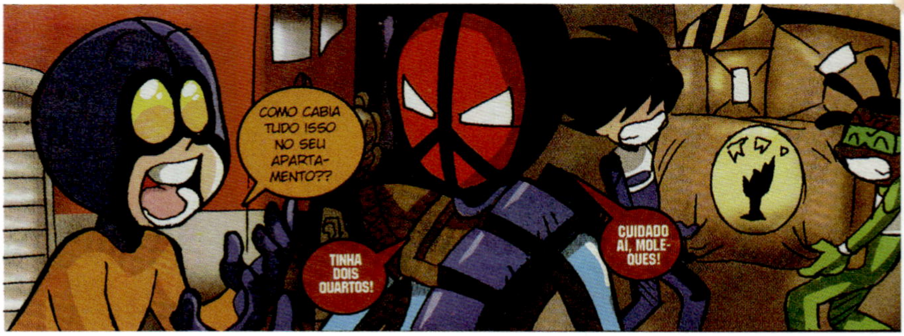
COMO CABIA TUDO ISSO NO SEU APARTA-MENTO??
TINHA DOIS QUARTOS!
CUIDADO AI, MOLE-QUES!

More art from Paulo's work on COMBO RANGERS

video games and I play guitar and sing in a hard rock trio called "Octane" in Brazil. You can find us on MySpace and YouTube. As far as my favorite groups go, I like Avenged Sevenfold, Story of the Year, and System of a Down. From the "Old School" I love Iron Maiden and Metallica. I also like pop and classical music. I love Beethoven, Bach, and Mozart. I don't understand classical music, but I appreciate it so much. I like some Brazilian pop music but I really dislike, (I don't want to say hate, it's a strong word)... SAMBA! Samba's the national music of Brazil. It's upbeat and encourages listeners to dance. It's not for me, though.

So all of you who may have questions for me, please post them on the Papercutz Blog and I'll try to answer as quickly as possible! My favorite titles from THE HARDY BOYS so far are #8: "A Hardy Day's Night" (just a beautiful father and son story) and #15: "Live Free, Die Hardy!" which was action-packed. I've got to thank Jim Salicrup, Terry Nantier, Scott Lobdell, Laurie E. Smith, and Mark Lerer for all of their hard work and support. Perhaps most importantly: thanks to THE HARDY BOYS fans! Without you we wouldn't be able to put these great graphic novels together. Thanks and be sure to ask me questions!

– 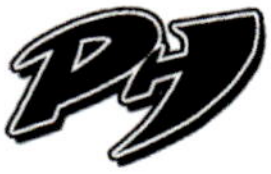